ASK AT THE UNICORN

ASK AT THE UNICORN

Norman Thomas

A NEW DIRECTIONS BOOK

For
Alice

ASK AT THE UNICORN

CHAPTER ONE

AT FIRST it seems the same. Dawn comes, voices are heard, people appear, commerce begins, is carried on and dies down. Music fades in and love begins. But before night falls the coloured mirrors spin and the language is no more the one you know. The signs in the shop windows are not the same. There are no yellow cabs and no red and blue mail boxes. A corner is turned and signposts point to unknown places.

Colour changes and smells change; clouds move differently. The rivers and the streams and the winds and the rain use an archaic speech.

It was a long way to come and a long time to look for a man who might never have been there.

A hand across the window made a hole in the vapour and when he looked through the glass was cold to his face. The storm slow-beaded rain across the windows and dark arms of trees came out of the night to wave at the carriage lights. The train trundled along the cliffs towards the end of land, the sea's commotion lost. The thunder was muffled but the lightning near and hopping from hill to hill on stiff legs.

The train turned from the sea, gathered speed and shuddered when the iron clamps went down. The lights trembled and yellowed. From the country around came no light from farmhouse or cottage or village: the country-side was forsaken by everything but the night. The train slowed, the wheels not now screaming, and then stopped. There was a singing from the steam-hot pipes under the seats and a steady tapping from the rain on the roof. Morgan drained his flask and slipped it into his inside pocket with his flute.

The door swung open.

'Come on out then into the night,' the old man said. With his lantern low he in a green light with the red to the right.

The wind dropped and steam boiled up before him obscuring all but his face with one blind eye in a bubble of skin and one eye opened wide.

'End of the world?' Morgan shouted, picking up his bag.

'Dyfnaint. This is Dyfnaint,' said the old man.

Dyfnaint. The dark valley.

The old man spoke again but the wind came and blew the words around his mouth and across his cheek and away into the storm. All the elements in a noisy night were there in welcome. Morgan turned up his collar and stepped down into the whip of the wind. No one else got off—no one else was on. The carriage door clanged. The old man walked away, his lantern swinging; the green light turned to crimson and a thin whistle went up like a shrieking bat. The train creaked, then chuckled evilly away.

The shape of the night dark dancing to the rain and in the sky lighter moving forms as cloud piled up and fell over cloud. Engine sparks settling near the house-warmed windows. A lamp, gas lit, went fluttering like a burning bird lighting only its falling air. Another light in its cradle above a gate shone on a shelter, blown down but held by a taut wet rope, its corrugated wings scraping and clanging as the wind clung. An empty milk churn rolled in a rainblack hollow.

'Can you . . .'

But the old man could not, being inside with the door closed.

('And there he was—gone.' Grando used to say it.)

It said WAY OUT on the gate but it looked more like the way in to a place he'd rather miss. The path, unpaved and running with water, dipped down by a crazy bush to a large tree and a rough road. The wind wet-smacked the trousers to his legs and water trickled down his neck. He started down the path, his feet sliding in the mud.

Half-way down the night stopped. A blue flame burnt the air and ran down the tree, cracking it. Before his hands were over his face he saw branches against the sky and as he fell there was a crashing all about him and there were noises like demons. When the noise was over he lay still, a singing in his ears and water running under his hands, until his breath was steady. One side of his face was burning and his arm was numb. He touched his face and knew there was blood. He struggled up through the branches and, leaving his bag, scrambled up the path and to the house. Another flash and the rain came swirling, and when the thunder cracked it shook the roots of the trees and shuddered the door. Morgan knocked and the door opened a hand's width.

Around the edge of the door the stationmaster reached and pulled him in. 'Bang,' the old man said, 'and the world fell out of bed.'

The room was warm and Morgan's tension eased.

'Act one, scene two,' he said, rubbing the rain from his hair. 'A house near hell or thereabouts.'

'My house is the mirror of my mind.'

'Crazy,' Morgan said, grinning. San Francisco was never like this. Turn over and dream some more.

A grey bigpregnant cat like a fur bowler hat stared from a pile of blankets on a brass bedstead, and a fluffed-up-in-itself speaking-to-itself bird in a fire-corner cage suddenly went wheewheeetoowhee frightening itself so that it huddled low and closed its grey lids.

'Storms are like churchbells,' the old man said as the thunder came again.

'This one tolled for me.' He rubbed his arm and worked his fingers. 'That oak tree was manic.' He did a quick pantomime.

'The big oak fell? So, it was an old tree.' He peered with his one good eye at Morgan's face and probed with two crooked fingers at the scratch.

'It is nothing,' he said, turning to the fireplace and pouring water from a kettle into an enamelled bowl. 'Take off your coat and trousers.'

Morgan did so, looking them over and flicking a hand at the mudstreaks. The cut tingled when he swished water over his face.

'People fear and worship storms,' said the old man as he hung Morgan's trousers over a chair. 'Storms change the land and upturn trees to show twisted roots like turtle legs waving at the wind. The roots look naked as the things of the tree which sustain its truth are plucked away like twisting leeches before a flame. Plucked away and flicked away as the tumbling bushes over and over go into the swollen rivers and to the sea.' He offered a ragged towel.

12

'Soap in my ears,' Morgan said with a grin. (From far back he heard—'It's easier not to listen, Charlie. That way you never get offended and you never get confused.') He rubbed his face and squatted before the fire to warm his arse. 'I'll keep it formal,' he said, fingering his tie.

Religious-red curtains swirled out like a cape where two lights touched each other and retreated—a soft yellow light from an inverted tear of gas, lampbrass shining, and, where it faded, a glow from between the black arms of the grate where they crossed as at a bailiff's belly. The floor under and around the table was in darkness and things, containers, bundles, bottles resided there. Things packed up, contained and waiting there. Where the weak light fell over the table-cloth fringe it smoothed a worn carpet, dark colours swirling like a scene from a glass aquarium roof above tails and tentacles.

A circle with a dark rim—a storm moon—lighted the ceiling sky. A tall clock knocked out noises with a squeak and a squeal of works and the shuteyed bird spoke to it.

Morgan sat in the chair offered to him and crossed his legs, his shirt ends reaching for his knees. The stationmaster tenderly moved the pregnant cat and sat on the bed. His face was grey with white wrinkles at the lighted eye and red around the bubble of skin, with stubble around a drooping moustache. His hands clasped and each thumb came around to rub the other. Below his trouser cuffs dirty flannel pyjamas pink and white and above his opened boots his ankles were grimed.

'I'm looking for a man,' Morgan finally said.

Without taking his eye from the fire the old man said, 'Everyone comes looking for something.'

'His name is Rhydderch.'

'I do not know a Rhydderch, but you could ask at the *Unicorn*.'

'I do not know a Rhydderch! Everywhere I go no one knows a Rhydderch. Or if they do it isn't the one. Did you ever talk to yourself to the point where to get back to where you started from you can just as easy go all the way round? And all the time you know it's a waste.'

'There are not many who think that there is much of value here.'

'I bet the gravediggers have a strong union.'

There was a long pause and then, softly at first with the wind whining and the thunder break seeming to wait for the end of the line, the old man spoke.

'One day in the spring of my life my father, my mother and I went up Black Mountain. Went up Black Mountain. We went up Black Mountain in the spring of the year at dusk with stars appearing. My father said look boyo a fire is lit and my mother said hush too young he is to focus his eyes but I saw the flames like reflected light in a boy's eye far-off below across two valleys. Larger licked the flames and my mother said she saw a flame all alone go up to heaven . . . It was a man burning the body of his child and a crowd of thousands watched excited and with fear and oh so shocked they were. Say his name was Price—a famous man he was but names I forget—a big man in a red coat with a foxtail hat—say his name was Price, well Jesus Price was his son and Mary Price was his daughter. Both were burned, the first they were I think ever to. He wore a foxtail cap and a scarlet coat. My grandma knew him well.'

Coal borne upon wood fell sparking to the fire and frightened the green and yellow bird.

'When I was eight,' the old man said, 'I saw a boy fall,

14

in full sight, off the bright side of the mountain, and yet they found him on the sand in the clear pool with no marks, like sleeping there, his face on the water-rippled sand. And no one would believe I saw him fall . . .

'You will see things in Dyfnaint that you saw years ago and new things you will see though they have been present all the time. You come back on tradition but leave tradition and the smell of brimstone comes on the wind. And always there is wind. Three hairs on the chest of a woman and she is burnt as a witch . . . There could be little people stuck with pins . . . A daughter quiet with eyes so dark and skin so white was born of father and his daughter. It was kept a creature mute by daughter's mother . . . and father was killed by daughter . . . Now the daughter lives with creatures only she can see.'

With deep breathing and slow settling there was a long quiet, but sad.

'A man came to Dyfnaint captive, stayed a farmer. The wife he took was young and straight but he being different she turned slut, hateful of her people, fearful of her man. Once a prince he descended to the level of our people and sank below and was nothing . . . Then they had a child, a boy beautiful with the joy of life. His voice was like the doves and like the nightingales; his smile was like the sun. And his cheeks were full like an autumn squirrel . . . And seeing what they had produced in their tick of truth they pulled themselves up by their lust and loved again. He is a good man and a good farmer. She sees him clearly and they kiss life as it rushes by. The good people like them and the rest they see only as they see passing sickness . . .

'Up on the mountain there is a snake coiled through two acres, stepping stones from tip to tail, with dotted eyes and tongue set down the valley to the woods. Once within its coil was an altar and is still a stone which rocks with the wind. Blood is dry now but below—not on the hill but in the trees—night is worshipped with all the turning over of the spirit as of the light . . . I know because I can remember . . . Will you have some tea?'

Morgan said yes. With thick-knuckled thin hands the stationmaster took down a fat brown teapot and placed it near the fire to warm. There was another crash of thunder but it was the storm's death. The cat and the bird made movements as if dismissing the day and preparing for sleep.

He poked the fire and the singing changed and a wisp of steam went up and soot fingers on the side of the kettle flexed in the flames.

Morgan tried his trousers, and, finding them almost dry, he put them on, but he unbuttoned his shirt and pulled at his tie.

'All this,' he said, 'is this Dyfnaint?'

'Oh yes. This is Wales. There are cities in Wales but I do not know cities.' From a five-sided canister with blue herons drifting over dripping trees he measured the tea, lifting it close to his face, smelling it. After the pouring into the thin cups he sprinkled some crumbling herbs with a horny thumb and finger.

'I know cities,' said Morgan. 'That's all I know.'

'What are cities?' With both hands the old man held his cup and sipped, not looking at him.

And it came to Morgan with no trouble at all.

'The centre of my city came up through the Chinese Church of the Nazarene,' he said. 'I had a place above it on the top floor—a view always acts nice on a woman's system.

16

Used to take them to the roof to look at the lights on the bridge and on the hills and on the boats coming and going. There was always a lousy smell of boiled crab and geraniums and Diesel oil. Cold too, but poetic.

'On one side of my place was a stripper and her man who played bad trumpet. On the other a bum who used to teach economics in Iran. Whenever he got drunk he thought he was in a prayer tower—you could hear him for eight blocks. Across the back stairway were a couple of whores and their kids: their bed was so large it had to be pulleyed up through the bay window. Either business was bad or they loved their work too much for they skipped owing six months rent. In that building were all kinds in three major colours working through various stages of social complications.'

The old man nodded, as if eager.

'Sundays were bad though with pure Chinese voices coming up through a haze of Saturday night with *Onward Chlistian Soldier*. The bells of a church like a movie house always went flat on Sundays. I wrote to the Pope, but he didn't do anything about it.' Morgan slid down into the musty cushions and lifted a leg over the arm of a chair. He toughened his voice some.

'Saturdays were better,' he went on. 'All afternoon a babel of Italian, Chinese and Filipino voices with "youbet" and "damright" and "bullshit" interspersed so you could follow the trend of thought. When the lights came on the population changed over. I used to split my roll and put hills into every pocket in the hope I might forget one of them and end the night with enough for Wheaties.' The toughness wouldn't stay. 'There used to be a man, black as loneliness —he'd see me coming. He had a red-lined cape and a top hat. No, his name wasn't Price—it was How-Much. He'd whisper things and hold the door drape aside to make me stop. But it was only a tired woman with feather-stuck nipples and a butt-cutting string, and a man on drums who thought he was making cement.

'Round and round and drink a drop and in and out of places, and there'd be a time when you're reading Ovid pasted to the door of the men's room and wondering whether the guy next to you has made a mistake and should be in the ladies. In the bar lots of words going around working up an excitement for those who tried and failed, and showing contempt for those who tried, gave up and gave in to success. Inventing a new language—a feeling language with new words. "What's new?" and then trying to prove the answer. Guys who want to be in touch with the times so they reject the good old for the bad new because it was too tough to tell the bad new from the good new.

'So you add your dimesworth. You find out what's doing, who's doing who. You listen to lies and rumours, you deadpan the book and jazz reviews, you make a few passes and fend off a couple, you get into a discussion and before you can scratch your kalinkas there's a beer or a thumb in your eye. But there's always a good woman and you find her and there you are laughing at the price of eggs. Drunk. Glorious. And you stick with her and the night is made.'

He poured more tea, as if he owned the place.

'Six o'clock in the morning—getting from a taxi at Pier 23 for no good reason and walking in the morning wet, kicking cigar butts and crumpled packs, listening to the fog horns and watching the swishing street cleaners. The girl with crooked lipstick and sticky hair but with a gone smile. And you gulp the coffee to cover up all that goddamn trembling.

'Maybe the city I know is just a string of Saturday nights. I guess there were other nights, but I don't remember them so well.

'Being alone in an allnight place breaking Saltines into a bowl of chili: with an empty feeling and not knowing of a thing you need to do . . . Sitting with a man who's got it and it's all coming out and you say "Keep mine too" and you don't come in when you're supposed to so he stays with it and you grin, "By God—you mother—where'd you find it?" and he wipes the spittle from his reed and scratches his black nose and says "It just came man—boop boop". Then you wish you could keep it awhile.

'You know, it's looking for jobs. Playing flute for Chico, driving a cab, lifting boxes, making stained glass, selling books or Blue Cross, adding up figures handing out tickets punching numbers—you know. It's beggars hailing buses then not getting on them, drunks falling from cable cars, cops peering into shutdown shops, black trucks picking up sleepers who've wet their pants. It's a woman throwing you a show and it's laughing when she starts to cry because she needs the money. Sure it's a turning away from a man with a friendly face—but who wants a kiss in the ear?

'A girl I never liked said it's like a smooth coat covering the hot skin of humanity and there are holes in the coat and when you run an aimless hand over the coat you get the tingles.'

It had come out with no censorship but now he knew it had turned to just words. 'She tried to sell it to Herb Caen,' he muttered. He picked up his cup and drank. This stuff didn't come in tea bags.

'Are we talking to each other?' he asked.

'Indeed, oh indeed.' The old man wiped his tea-wet

19

moustache with the back of his hand. 'I cannot understand two words together but it is valid. Oh indeed, indeed.'

'No, I've been putting on a pitch. We're just agreeing. That's bad, man.' He grinned, falling into an act. 'No point in pissing in the bath—we'll just get a ripple of enthusiasm with no foam. And it's unsanitary. A city isn't like what I've said. It's much more than I've said.'

'Yet you come to Wales,' said the old man.

'A man makes mistakes. Sometimes you think you're onto something solid.'

The old man picked up a thin taper of burnt wood which had fallen onto the tarnished brass fender when he had blown on the fire. He placed it on his hard hand, showing it to Morgan.

'What does that look like?'

Morgan said, 'Like an insect's wing.'

'That is what it is. I am glad you came. I hope you stay.'

Then he turned his hand over and the insect's wing fluttered to the floor. The back of his hand was soft with a sheen above the movements of blood and sinew like ice over turning water.

'You are young,' he said. Then, 'Perhaps spring will come.'

'So—spring you've heard of?'

'Seasons do not come of their own accord. Someone has to bring the spring.'

'Well it didn't come with me.' Morgan stood up and put on his coat. 'How do I find the village?'

'Follow the road.'

'I guess so. But right or left?'

'Left. Right goes nowhere. Past the house of the preacher. If you are lost he is no help at all. He likes Dyfnaint because he believes in the devil. One day he hopes to believe in God.'

'A man with ambition.'

'On again is the inn. You are going to the inn?'

'Have I a choice?'

'Not if you are a stranger. I can give you a lamp.'

'Thanks.'

'It is a red one for searching for the devil.'

He took a dusty and smoke-blackened lamp from beneath the table and lifted the glass. He trimmed the wick and lit a taper from the fire and the dust burnt with a smell of brimstone. The flame was a blue bubble hanging like dew on dandelion fuzz. He fiddled and the bubble changed shape, became flat like another room's escaping light, then high and falling in a liquid form. But only a red glimmer shone through the dusty windows. A curl of smoke browned and burnt out. Across the lantern's face the stationmaster drew his thumb again and again, the red paint rippling under his nail in lines which joined and crossed until there was a yellow light with rosy edges.

'Come back in a few days and see the kittens,' he said, handing over the lamp.

'Right. On my way home.'

The old man was bending over the cat, smoothing with careful hands her bulging belly and she stretched her head up and against his arm.

'Her eyes, I always think,' he said, 'are like children's sweets which fill the mouth with hard sucking satisfaction as they change from yellow to black.'

(Didn't he ramble though!) Morgan touched the doorknob and the cat jerked her head around as if scared but straight away went to work washing her foot. The old man straightened stiffly and opened the door. The wind had dropped but the rain still fell. Morgan stepped out into the night with the dark tugging at his coat.

'Thanks a lot,' he said. 'See you.'

'Don't go alone,' came the answer.

The door closed.

The light from the lantern streamed out on the rain into shadows in the night. A red mist on the raintamping, the rain red like nails, and the platform deep red and the air rose red and a light over the gate. Two lights—he one, the gate the other. The night looking down with its swollen cheeks about to spit.

With the aid of the lantern he found his bag under the branches of the stricken tree, and with difficulty pushed his way through to the road, where he turned left.

He could see no houses but, walking on, he saw a weak wavering point of light coming along the ridge ahead. Nearer, then, against the lighter west sky, he saw a man hunched on a bicycle, head down against the rain and his fear. Along he came on his devious path, the beam flicking here and there as if away from, never towards, the way before him. Half-turning with the cat's-eye slit of light going away, the bicycle stopped and the hunched figure un-hunched to a tall thin shape. A gate creaked.

Then a cry. A half-gasping help-crying god-complaining call and a clatter as the bicycle fell and the cat's-eye danced and from the ground pointed up at a yellow face pitted with dark eyes and puckered with a teeth-lost mirth-lost mouth. Then the man was gone—up the path and into the house. Morgan went on and to the path, put down his bag and leaned on the gate. No lights went on. Perhaps peeping from a window.

'Hoho!' Morgan cried, holding out his arms. 'Beds not slept in, soup not blown on,' he intoned. 'Rooms forgotten. Blackbird soot from chimneys full and lamps not lit, doors unopened . . .

'Bread not broken, wine not sipped. Not in this house, this dark castle to praise my dark Welsh god.'

He took out his flute and played a low tune.

> *Ah poor bird . . . take thy flight . . .*
> *far into the so–or–rows of this dark night . . .*
> *Ah poor bird take thy flight . . .*
> > *Ah poor bird*
> > *Ah poor bird.*

'Crazy,' Morgan said aloud, shaking his head. He turned and picked up his bag and lantern.

From the ridge he could see a huddle of lights, the calm harbour dark, and the straggling cottage lights going along the spit of land to the thump and the white fury of the sea.

CHAPTER TWO

HE CLOSED the outer door behind him, BAR black and backwards on a dappled glass, cool on fingertips; the tiled floor red and black, and reddest and blackest in the rainsplash beneath the door. Pissoir-green passage walls leaned up into a dark shaft balanced above banisters and stairs. In a glass cage crouched a dull-eyed fox and a bird with painted blood. From under the bar door an old voice came out on an edge of light but no warmth or welcome came with it.

Morgan opened the inner door and the Welsh voice crackled into silence. An old prune of a man clutching a large brass watch on a long brass chain looked up with frightened eyes and hunched forward in his chimney seat. His pimpled, purple neighbour in a tight black coat spat into the fire. A round man in a striped shirt with a metal stud greening his throat was standing on a chair, fiddling with a bulb in an ornate electric fixture. The light came from an oil lamp on the table.

'G'evening,' the round man said. The others did not speak. A lean sheepdog bitch with bright red dugs wagged at

24

Morgan and struggled up to go to him when he clipped his fingers, but the old prune of a man snarled gerback.

A glass put down went bang, breathing became self-conscious, and drip-drops of water echoed behind the bar. Three amber bottles on a shelf looked on like eyes. Greetings like a welcome to a wake.

'Good evening,' Morgan said and nodded to the two men in the chimney seat. They looked away from him, nodding and mumbling a good evening.

'Off the train you are?' asked the publican.

'Yes. I'd like a room.'

The publican got down from the chair holding the light bulb as if in wonder. He peered at it, shook it near his ear, then, in indecision, placed it next to a curling sandwich under a belljar.

'It's a bit early in the year,' he said, dusting the tips of his fingers together.

'Let me have a whisky while you're thinking about it,' Morgan said.

The publican poured, then waited, the open bottle in his hand. A grin trembled but hung on. Morgan gave a here's-how with his glass and drank. The man in black sank the last of his beer and came up to the bar in a limping hurry. Morgan feigned preoccupation with a poster announcing (but gone by) 'A Performance of Bach's Passion according to St Matthew in the Slaughter-house Field'.

He motioned for another nip and when it was poured he went to the fireplace and leaned against the mantelpiece. The publican wiggled his nose then probed a thumb into his nostril until he found what was bothering him. He rolled it into a ball but had trouble flicking it away.

'Just not prepared for visitors, see,' he said.

'Don't worry about it,' Morgan said. 'I'll find something.' Gingerly he sat on the edge of the chair, his trousers cold against his legs.

'I will go and see the wife,' said the publican, setting down the bottle and leaving, scratching behind his ear with the cork.

From the corner of his eye Morgan saw the man in black lift the bottle and take a quick swig but he caught his tongue in the opening and it came away with a bottled plop, and in his haste he banged the bottle back down on the bar. Involuntarily Morgan grinned and turned to the man. But the man scowled and spoke in Welsh to his companion who replied in Welsh.

The bitch was whining and pawing at a pile of firewood and with relief they all gave her their attention. A spider, drawn in with curled legs in a corner of a log was showing just enough life to excite her. She barked, her ears arched like eyebrows, and as her master got up she turned eagerly and the spider scurried into shadow.

'Spiders! Unnatural, dirty creatures,' sputtered the dried, spitting man. 'Why they exist I do not know. Ugly they are and serve no use at all.' Yet he fumbled with the logs. With the logs away the spider flattened itself and the man partly crushed it between his fingers, and made noises of disgust as he held it with yellow muck squashed under his thumbnail. He rubbed it off over the fire and it dropped onto an unburned log, writhing as it was held by a mashed part of itself.

Going back to his seat the man gave a quick, proud polish to his fingernails on his waistcoat.

The bitch went to Morgan on her stomach and he rested a hand on her pretty head.

Hallelujah! he sang to himself, but sadly.

The publican returned and said, 'We can let you have a room for thirty shillings bed and breakfast.' Adding, to Morgan's nod, 'Unless it is longer you will be staying.'

'Let's talk about it in the morning.'

'Very well, sir.'

Bribery past, Morgan said, 'Have a drink with me,' including the other men in his invitation.

Behind the bar were two barrels, one tilted by a chain and pulley, each with a wooden tap in the bunghole, but the publican ignored them and poured three more drinks from the bottle.

'Still raining is it?' shouted the bitch's master with a ferocious look at Morgan.

'Yes,' said Morgan.

'Well then!'

'A big storm it is. 'Lectric line is down,' said the publican, with a proud smile.

'The big tree near the railroad too,' said Morgan.

'Aye?' said one.

'God!' said the other.

The bitch whimpered so he scratched her and she nuzzled his hand. The men smacked their lips and sighed as they put down their glasses.

'Rain, rain,' said one.

'Aye,' said the other.

'Is it on holidays you are?' asked the barman.

'I'm looking for a man named Rhydderch.'

'Rhydderch, Rhydderch,' they all sang together, looking in lost wonder at each other and shaking their heads. Still puckering their mouths for the last of the liquor.

'I guess I'm on the wrong road,' Morgan said.

'Rhydderch, Rhydderch,' went the dirge, and then a querulous solo from the pimpled man in black. 'Not a copper are you?'

Morgan shook his head. 'Who'd be the best man to ask?' But they said they did not know.

Footsteps sounded and the door opened, but Morgan did not turn then.

'Er—Mr er—what is it your name is?' asked the publican.

'Morgan Johns.'

'Welsh name you've got.'

'Born here in Wales I was,' said Morgan in an attempt at the accent.

'Well well indeed! Gwylan,' he said to the woman moving away from the door, 'take Mr Johns upstairs will you.' Then, in explanation, he shouted, 'She will take you to your room.'

Morgan went out into the passageway and a woman with brown skin and dark eyes was waiting on the stairs. ('See, there was this salesman who stopped at this inn and . . .') She carried sheets and held a lamp high to light the way. Morgan followed her. Her backside tilted from one step to another pulling her skirt up on her full hips. Her legs were heavy but with shape and with small ankles and a hollow at the knee like a seawet cave.

On the first landing he said, 'You the wife?' She tossed her head with a 'Hah!' ('. . . and there was no room for this salesman except a bed in the . . .') She wore a man's shirt but her lips were bright.

On the second landing she opened a door and went into the dark of the room, shadows racing before her to the curtains and the corners.

After setting down the lamp and pulling the curtains she turned to him as if for his reactions. Morgan looked around

28

and shook his head. It was a small room, chill, with dark, skull-like roses on the wall.

'Pooh! Who died?'

'It has been closed all winter.'

'It should have been boarded up and a cross chalked on the door.'

She laughed and dropped the sheets on the bed, kicking the chamber pot as she did so and the laughter continued so Morgan turned to watch her. Her tongue spun all over her mouth, wetting her lips. Her laugh was low and nicely vulgar and her eyes jigged with reflected light.

'Would you like a fire?' she asked.

'How else could I stand it.'

'He will charge you for it.'

'What about the spiders and the mice?'

'Free they are.' Her hands were on her hips and her breasts were full like fruit. But it did not bother him at all. ('I don't want to hear any of your salesman jokes.')

'You look like a wet mole,' she said.

'In a mole's hole.'

She stepped close and looked at the cut on his face and then at the mud on his sleeve, but she said nothing. He remembered his sore arm but when he moved it it was easier. She turned and stooped at the fireplace, adding sea-smoothed logs to the pile of yellowed newspaper and small sticks.

'Do you have a light?' she asked, and he tossed her a match-box. There was a green splurt from the match then a slow growth of light. The pale flames spread with a whisper across the mouth of the fireplace. Staying crouched she spoke over her shoulder. 'Why not go down into the warm until the fire is going?'

29

'I'd like to get used to it while I've got company,' he said, pressing down on the sagging bed. 'I'm the nervous type.'

'I see you do not like the room?'

'It's just that I don't believe it.'

A crackled and yellowed mirror tilted on the wall reflecting feet and the eagles' claws on the legs of the chairs. The room was not dark from lack of light; it made its own gloom. Over the fireplace was an etching of two lonely-looking women feeding doves, and on another wall a misty picture suggesting a flagellation. Paper booped out with the damp.

'We lease you an area of our unhappiness for we are employed for your discomfort,' he said, as if reading a sign. She got up and moved the lamp to the mantelpiece, putting less of the room in shadow. Then she placed an iron screen against the fire.

'That's to draw the flames,' she said. 'I will bring you something to eat.'

'Forget it—but I could use more of this.' He handed her the flask, tapping the Scotch tag.

'Are you staying long, Mr Johns?' she asked.

'Tomorrow too soon?'

'I'll fill your flask.'

He put out his arm to stop her. 'It's been a crazy day,' he said.

She nodded and went to the door.

Some days are made of silver . . . (don't go—but she was gone) . . . and some are made of brass.

Elbows on knees he held his fingers against his eyes, feeling their curve. There was a twitching, and a dark moving pattern behind his lids, the colours changing but

30

the pattern always the same. Things come back, whether beckoned or not; good things and things sooner forgotten. And they decide the day.

> *The night of storm will never end for me:*
> *The dawn is lost, and sunk beneath the sea.*

We remember too much, he said almost aloud. Then, to hear his voice, 'What a grave!'

He huh-ed a few times, surprised that no mist appeared. Water had seeped into his bag so he emptied it and stood it near the fire. He took off his shoes and socks and changed his pants and shirt, and rubbed his damp feet with a clean sheet.

The fire suddenly roared in the chimney so he took away the screen. Adding what was left of the wood he crouched for a while before the fire, his eyes held by the blue and green flames. Then he shook himself and stood up, taking out the flute. When the tap came at the door he was sitting in a chair near the fire with his feet up, silently blowing across the mouthpiece.

He said come-in and the door opened and the woman stood there with the fire red in her eyes. Her thighs swelled like a lizard's tail with a shallow pout where they joined in shadow. She picked up a small coal bucket and turned the tray onto her hip as she kicked the door shut.

He inclined his head and opened a palm in welcome.

She said, 'Pritchard thinks a fire and food pampers a man . . .'

'So what's wrong with excess?'

'. . . he thinks a man is safe when he is cold and waiting for food . . .'

'Who wants to be safe?'

'Pritchard.'

'God bless him.'

'That's why he is angry.'

It was silly, like a play—dip-dap-doh went the back and fore of talk like fun.

'I thought I said I wasn't hungry.' The flask, he saw, had been filled.

'I know.'

'I probably need it. I always say no when I'm not sure whether or not I want something.'

She laughed and two lizard tongues of fire danced in her eyes.

'What's that for?' she asked, looking at the flute in his lap.

'For blowing,' he said, and blew her a long run.

'Salvation Army type,' she said.

'Salvation Army retired, ex-carnival and circus. I'm a yardbird. Charlie is me darlin'.'

She looked as if in disbelief.

'No,' he said, waving a lighted match as if to set fire to someone, and only lighting his cigarette on an afterthought. 'I play around but it's not my life. Jazz on the flute is a passing fancy. Knitting music is what you're paid for. I do anything that pays a couple of bucks.'

She added coal to the fire, then brought a small table near him and put the tray on it. There was red cheese and a lamb-chop and pickled onions and brown bread, and butter water-speckled with the salt, and a steaming stone pot.

'He would not let me prepare you anything warm but there is hot chocolate.'

'Hot chocolate! I haven't had hot chocolate for twenty years.'

The knock on the door was imperious, and in came the

landlord. 'Must ask you not to play any musical instrument here,' he said. 'Entertainments tax you know.'

'Who's playing?' The little fat man seemed to jump up and down in the flickering light.

'Heard you I did, sir. No more please.'

'Oh that—I farted,' said Morgan.

The round man sputtered. 'Sir, ladies present.'

'And to you, sir, how does a woman differ from a man?' He'd never get that up-and-down accent back.

The publican stepped back, glared at the girl, and mumbled, 'No more please,' and left, leaving the door ajar.

'What's with him?' Morgan asked, but she was busy with a pillow slip, her back to him. 'You know,' he went on, 'a remarkable instrument called a thumb has been fashioned. Without it you couldn't play the flute or pick up a pickle, and all Pritchard can find to do with it is stick it up his nose. If he was naked he'd have a conflict.' She still said nothing. 'Lord, I'm tired . . . am I getting you into trouble?'

'Don't fret,' she said.

Morgan poked a finger at a heat blister on the varnished mantelpiece. He picked a flake off and dropped it in the fire then smelled his fingers. The old smell made him frown.

'Sit down and eat,' she said.

'Hot chocolate,' he muttered. He poured some from the jug but after sipping it he added to it from the flask. She nodded to his offer and he poured some whisky into the cup-cap, and she drank it down with a shiver and a gasp.

'You must be rich,' she said.

'This is a necessary expense,' he said. She shook her head to the offer of more and turned back to the making of the bed.

Morgan broke off some cheese and buttered the heavy

33

bread; the salt came in a chunk chipped from a block and he sprinkled some over his meat. As he ate he watched her flip the sheets and deftly guide their fall. She, aware of his eyes upon her, did everything slowly so that she would not be all thumbs and feet.

'I heard Pritchard call your name,' he said, 'but I couldn't understand it.'

'It is Gwylan.'

'It's got a nice sound.'

'It means seagull.'

'It's the first time I've seen a captive seagull.'

'You are not seeing one now.'

'You work long hours,' he said.

'I'm off again and on again.'

'Are you off finally when you finish making my bed?'

'Almost. A few more things.'

'Would you come for a cigarette and a talk?' he asked.

She turned down the sheet, smoothed the covers, then turned to him with her arms folded and one hip stuck out.

Morgan shook his head. 'Just look at me. I'm in no shape to chase you round the room.'

She bent to pour the rest of the chocolate, and her shirt fell away from a sweet valley; her flesh was textured red. 'I am not afraid of you,' she said, her accent heavy and melodious. 'I was just thinking how different you are from the men of Dyfnaint. Different also from the other American we had at the *Unicorn*. Glad I will be to talk with you.' She went to the door. 'Can I come in without knocking?'

'Sure.'

'For if they hear me they will not like it.'

When she left, the room took over with its noises. There

was a creaking of windows and a banging of the door in its frame, and the fire spat and roared in the chimney. From outside came the soft singing of the wind and the rhythmic squeaking of the *Unicorn* sign. Yet in the *sotto voce* tumult came a cry of silence to hint of change: then sound and silence pulled themselves back and forth over the ridge of the house, producing music. But unfamiliar was the music, nothing like churchbells for there was no order. At least, none that was apparent.

Warm now, he felt the lines fade from his face. When he had finished eating he stretched out.

Wales was still the worst. Wales was drab, Wales was drear; even the sun did not know its way about Wales. Cut off by mountains, by sea, and by a stubborn superiority that would not hold up to a candle, the Welsh do not create anything, they do not manufacture much, they do not even say anything of any value. All they do is dig in the earth, chase sheep all over the mountains, play Rugby in the rain, and sing in a soulful manner. When they sing—what if there's no food in the house, or a pit explodes. That's tough! Leave the country? Why the world is Wales. The few who know there's another life go to London to show them how to do things, and when they've made their mark they're so pleased they become professional Welshmen and act outrageously while holding up their little tea-pinkies. This much he had learnt in the mining valleys.

Well this was it and more than enough. No more chasing clues of Grando—not after this week. Grando was old enough to be dead! Grando meant nothing now. Long ago there had been something but that had been some other man in some other time. Those memories were of innocence, of slow mornings waiting for miracles, and of nub-ends of days wondering whether the miracle had come and gone, unmarvelled at. And innocence has gone for good . . .

The door opened quietly and Gwylan was back, bringing with her the smell of apples. Without a word she closed the door and sat in the chair opposite. Morgan leaned over and offered her a cigarette which she took and waited, her hair held to one side, for him to strike the match.

'Players!' she said, letting the smoke drift from her mouth. 'I hoped they would be American cigarettes.'

'A weed's a weed.'

She slipped off her shoes and put her feet on the fire fender. 'They are talking about you downstairs,' she said. 'They say you are looking for someone.'

'Do I need a permit?'

'No one ever comes here just to see us.' At the O sound her mouth pouted out.

'I know. You don't get visitors in Wales—only strangers.'

'True,' she said, 'and the trouble with strangers is that they are so strange. They do not act as sensible people do.' Suddenly she seemed free from restraint and her words fell easily one over the other. 'They are always apt to do something unpredictable, and it is so embarrassing to witness someone doing what is so obviously not right. Strangers either bring too much that is new or they bring disaster.'

'I knew I was welcome,' he said, knowing he was.

'Americans are the worst. Always asking questions, always nosing around looking for things.' But there was a turning up of the mouth.

'What did the other American want?' Morgan asked.

'He was mourning the death of a poet. Mourning at the top of his voice, practising for a book he was going to write about it.' She shrugged. 'Poets are like milkmen in Wales.'

36

'Was he a good poet?'

'Yes. But the American, who said he was a poet also, kept talking big words with no meaning. He was like a man who was not content to sniff flowers or look at them or hold them under his girl's chin. He wanted to eat them, as a monkey would, separating the seeds with his nails and his front teeth and sucking on the petals. He was learning a tight BBC accent though he said pomes. He took me out because Uncle Caradoc-the-railway was the poet's friend, and because he had heard that I had been intimate—that was the word he used—intimate with the poet. All night long it was lah-de-dah questions.'

'I'm just looking for a man,' said Morgan.

'It must be important. Coming all the way from America.'

'I don't know whether it is. It's like getting up from a warm bed to go fumbling in the dark to meet a woman seen only in sleep. There you are, barely covered and with no one to meet, but because someone's watching you go through the motions. You look pretty damn dumb scratching your stomach at the gate to an empty road with no one coming. Same thing with promises; you're half-way around the world before you realize there's no one at the end of all that talk . . . Sometimes I think it's of no importance at all.'

'You do not look like a policeman, or a lawyer with a will.'

'I'm looking for a man my father knew. I knew him too, but then I was only a boy.'

'You liked him?'

'I guess,' he said.

'What was he like?'

'What d'you want—stories? Twenty years is a long time.' But he thought about it. 'All I'm sure of is his hairy

37

jacket and his brass-hooked boots, and his rasping chin. A long, untidy man, I remember, his pockets misshapen with apples and books. My mother didn't like him because when he started talking he'd walk around the room with his cup in his hand and he'd get excited and put it down on something polished. She also said he didn't wash often enough.' Morgan flipped his cigarette into the fire. 'He had a rich smell all right: he said it came from the stables. He took me down the pit once to see his pony. Going down in the cage I was scared and told him wild stories to cover up. He always listened to my stories as if he believed them . . . I called him Grando because he was like a spare grandad.'

'You are smiling,' she said.

'That was a long, long time ago. Smiles came once a week then, and looked like little silver coins that wouldn't buy much. How 'bout that! Now—well—you can't help liking crazy people.'

'My father is a bit crazy. Perhaps he can help you find your Grando.'

'I'd like to see him again.' He shrugged and shook something off. 'Not for my sake for we wouldn't have much to say to each other, but my old man—like now—the world's full of people taking messages to other people all over the place. You know—never speaking for themselves.' He grinned. (When you're in too deep—grin.)

A mouse scampered behind the wall until it came to the fireplace and there it stopped and scratched vigorously. Morgan, out of curiosity, tapped the wall with a shoe and the noise stopped. Then, sorry, he tapped again hoping to start it up again but the mouse stayed quiet.

'So your old man still lives in the village,' he said.

'Yes. William Williams-the-fish. Will Twice he is called.'

'I thought you lived in the pub.'

'I do.'

'Why don't you live with your old man?'

'You see? Americans always asking questions.' But she answered. 'There is only one big bed in Dada's house, and he likes to share it, sometimes, with a friend of mine.'

'You're considerate.'

'And this way it is not caught we are in each other's troubles.'

'Why don't you leave home?' he asked.

'Leave home? What do you mean?'

'What d'you mean what do I mean?'

'Leave home! That to me is almost a contradiction.' Her hands were spread over her hips, her thumbs against her belly which moved in and out with slow breathing. 'I suppose I understand. But, without a home—that would leave you like a hermit crab who goes around with a soft skin until he finds an empty shell in which to hide.'

'Do you think the world is one big home?'

'I am speaking of what I know. All I know is a few miles of coast . . .'

'Don't give me all the hills and the trees and the wind stuff because I've had about enough of it for one night. I can feel the fungus spreading between my toes.'

'This isn't Dyfnaint that assaults you,' she said. 'This is the last blow of winter. Is winter not like this where you come from?'

'You never want to leave to find out for yourself?'

'Indeed yes.'

'Assuming you know where your home is—you can't take it with you.'

'Home is where you happen to be.'

'Yeah.' He laughed and looked round the room, but, perhaps because he had been looking at the fire, he could not see the pictures on the wall, nor even the roses clearly.

'When you are about to move, Uncle Caradoc tells me,' she said, 'you must lay out everything you own, and decide what you have to take and what you have to leave behind. What you take is everything that makes the home you start with again. Is not that the way it is?'

'I brought my flute and some juice, and I left behind my long-johns. I'm not going to have much of a home in Wales.'

'I have often wondered whether the hermit crab really fits snugly into that hard shell.'

'I, never having seen one, wouldn't know.'

'At least he is protected, if that is what he wants. And there are always plenty of empty shells around.' Because the smile held something else, he dropped in a bit of flirting in self-defence.

'People in Wales are born with shells on,' he said.

'No, no,' she said. 'Thin skinned they are, and tempers they've got—as people find out. But you mean, I see, what holds me here.'

'Are you content?'

'No.'

'Then why not go someplace where you would be,' he said.

'Is discontent a place? I thought it was like a person. I was waiting to see why it is she is here.'

'Two-bit mystics wherever you go. You'd rather believe in ghosts than in central heating.'

'Indeed yes.'

'I'm glad I left when I did. Though you don't know it,

you're discontent because you've blood in your body that's never had a chance to thaw. Have you ever been away from Dyfnaint?'

'Now and then I go up to the city.'

'And do you like it?' he asked, just to keep it going. They were puffing up a bubble of warmth with shiny windows of her low voice, and his, and containing a fire and well-being and two people. A fine tension holding the walls taut.

'Once, in the city,' she said, 'I saw a man standing on a box at the corner of a park. Shouting and screaming by God, he was, that what this world needed was love. If all the people with hate in their heart could be destroyed, he said, the people who lived by love would remain happy. Once this was accomplished, there could be laws passed (and enforced by specially trained officers) governing the expression of hate; there would be education to ensure that all techniques of love were available to the rich and poor alike. "The sand of time is running out," he warned, his face red and contorted with emotion, "the time for decision is now. Sign the pledge that you will gird yourself for the supreme effort of love. Love or the world will crumble." I think he had a correspondence course. The petition went around and people signed it. People in the cities are wonders at signing petitions . . . Uncle Caradoc says you would need a flying horse and a magic trumpet to organize the people of Wales.'

'You can organize a morgue if the ice keeps up.' Then, laughing at himself, he said, 'A city rises with the sun on its walls so that, climbing out of the valley, you can see it like a great banner of leaves.' He made a tantarara gesture with his flute. 'White towers, white horses, coloured by silks or by the sun: statues, marble streets, courts with a golden light, men on horses, ships with sails—oh no low-down affair . . . you ever hear of a prince who lived outside the walls?'

'A city is put up by man to honour no one but himself,' she said.

'It is a refuge, that's what it is, from the dark, superstitious whimwhams. Signs and symbols sure, pretty and ornate, but placed high above the earth, touched only by the coming-on west wind.'

'Wonderful is the city for communication,' she went on with a smile. 'You can hear the news coming down the street, voices coming at you and bobbling past like a noisy cork, banners and signs and speakers. Wheels going round. Nothing there long enough to look at. Birds dull as dust there are but no beasts except the dogs who lead the blind.'

And there, of all places, she laughed.

Morgan, relaxed, saw Market all too clearly. She leaned forward onto her knees, her eyes heavy lidded. 'What did you ask me?'

'And do you like the city?' he asked, as if it had not been asked before.

'I like it, at times, for all the reasons I do not like it at others,' she said.

Down below came the sound of a closing door and cries, in Welsh, of goodnight.

Time was passing, peacefully, and was not always filled with talk. The fire had burned low once and Gwylan had added coal to it, and talk did not come again until it flared again. The fire was like a play and they were entertained by it, and time was consumed by it. Yet when the talk came around once more they picked up where they had left off.

'I was thinking how much I like the place I left,' Morgan said. 'I should have stayed there maybe. I guess it's a good thing people are different or they'd all be in the same place.' He unscrewed the cap of his flask and poured, stopping only when the cup was brimming. Lips pursed, he bent and sipped, then offered it to her.

She sipped and returned the cup, then pulled a cushion to the floor before the fire and sat on it with a comfortably curled back, her knees up and showing a long pale stretch of under leg. She scratched her thigh a little too much on the inside not to make him watch. Her shoulders were nudged forward and the light from the fire threw dark reds and yellows across her throat.

'I do never want to be where everyone else is,' she said. 'Sometimes I do not wish to leave; sometimes I want all the world to come to me a little bit at a time, bringing with it all its treasures . . .' Her eyes were bright and her mouth full and he could smell her like a collie in the sun. His hand went out to touch her but the motion was obvious so was stopped: resting his elbow on his knee he let his hand hang limp, the backs of his bent fingers almost against her wrist.

'Yet sometimes in the winter,' she said, her eyes fixed on the flames, 'when all this valley crouches under wind and snow, I wish I could go to another world where men are different. Where they have different shapes and habits and notions and beliefs; where all they have are mouths and eyes and organs and hands to please me, and all else that makes them up is new.' The touch of uncurled fingers upon her hand had been like the falling of one petal upon another— had he made the move or had the touch come to him? It was as if the fingers had acquired other senses and were savouring each other. Colour had come to her face.

43

'Then what would help you know the beautiful from the bad?' he asked.

Through her laughter she said, 'That, even now, I do not know. Animals they say never know these things. Nothing offends them. Neither beauty nor deformity. Is not that nice?'

Then it was he felt unsure.

They had been playing hide-and-seek, just missing each other's eyes, then following each other's gaze, knowing when the glance moves away from the cheek, waiting for it to travel to the hair, looking away before the eyes could meet. But now he broke it off.

'There is a book about the future,' he said, 'where all of mankind has been deformed, to some degree, by a fearful conflagration, and even there they have a standard of beauty below which one cannot expect to live. In this book man placates the devil by sacrificing those with more than the average share of disfigurement. So a man with eight fingers on one hand might be permitted to live but a woman with three rows of nipples would have to die.'

As if not hearing, she said, 'I would like to lie with a man from another star.'

Her face was in repose, her eyes closed as if in sleep: in sleep her lids were like anemones. With no movement she unfolded like a flower and there was a bloom to her skin, a light about her hair; her lips took on a dew. He felt her nearness like wings before him in the dark. He felt a warmth as when a cloud moves from the sun, a trembling as when the earth is shaken far away.

Her eyes opened and she permitted a wide look, deep down; an open face that bred uneasiness and brought up habit. Careful, with wide eyes watching, he put his hands

44

on her, and took his time about bringing her to him. Their mouths were full and met in gentleness; hers moved in pleasure. Breath from her nostril blew on his cheek and her fingertips were against his shirt. Then came a wave that almost took him. The smell of life with body heat, flesh against sweet flesh . . . But, careful . . . ! You are secure as long as you are remote. Love is a detached art that requires control . . . (Parenthetically, there was this bird in a tree and he was regular—came each day to sing a bit. Next thing it was breadcrumbs on a plate (he was fat as a cat—didn't need no breadcrumbs) hoping one day he'd be in your hand and you could stroke his feathers. How the hell close can you get to a bird anyway. What y'want to do with it? I dunno, Mac, just more than I'm doing now. Maybe a little silver chain, and he could sit on a perch while we serve the gin. Pretty bird like an olive? Yeah, he's ours. Neah, he likes it there) . . . There was a mist of down upon her cheek. Her mouth, warmed with a smile, was parted, and he knew a taste and smell of mingled smoke and liquor and womanliness. But don't be carried. Careful you don't bump noses or chinsies or she'll think you've never done it before . . . (Again, as before, there was this pleasure at looking at a coloured glass in a dismal place. You're going nowhere but pretty soon your head says 'Wonder what it's made of' and before you know it you've finished looking and you're up against the cold wall rubbing the glass and tapping it with a thumbnail. Next you're wondering how it's made, how much it cost, forgetting you ever enjoyed it.) . . . I am from another world . . .

Beneath his hands she moved, away but not apart from him. The bubble was still there holding the fire and them together but oh so fragile. She remained within his arm,

45

her hair against his mouth, but there was not complete agreement. She was more with something within herself than she was with him. As he was more with his pride than he was with her.

After a while she said, 'I hope you find Grando and I hope you stay a bit.'

'Whether or not I find him, I'll be gone in a week.'

'I am sorry. It would have done you and Dyfnaint good to know each other.'

Then they were still until a coal turned over and snuffed out its flame and all that was left was tinted smoke. The light from the lamp on the mantelpiece had lowered, and the wind at the window was almost gone.

The outer door closed downstairs and a bolt was shot into its socket. Morgan turned her to him again but she gave no hint, made no move, accepting what was offered. Afterwards she moved away and stood up.

'Tomorrow,' she said, 'go and see Willy Twice. If you will come with me now I will point out the way to his house.'

He did not move but she would not come back, so he slipped on his shoes and got up. In the hallway was no light, not even from the stair-well, but she took his hand and led him away from the head of the stairs. Down three steps and then up three, then she stopped and opened a door and led him into a room which had a female smell to it.

Still in the dark she took him to the window and from there he saw the pattern of lights.

'The last light around the harbour is where Willy lives...' but he interrupted, as if urgently, and they were together from thigh to mouth. Urgently, as if afraid of losing it, yet thinking all the time, resisting it.

There is an element, out of time, out of space, in which what you choose can become everything. And what you choose can be held through chaos or can be put away until there is time or place enough for the full appreciation of it. When it is held the acts of man seem incomprehensible and much of the world is like an indoor cowboy town with painted trees and clouds, and the sunshine comes from a hundred lights, and there is synthetic dust and emotions. When it is held man seems to be compelled by an unfamiliar script, and is far removed from the elements of earth and sky, and with no connection whatsoever with the other, as yet unnamed element.

From the yard below came a calling 'Kitty, kitty, kitty,' that went on, so he hung on to what he had chosen and together they turned to the window.

The clouds were breaking up and the sky was lit by the moon. Pritchard was at the door across the yard and as they watched the cat, tabby but black as the night till now, came and entered, its head up as it cried, and the door closed.

They could see into the kitchen where Mrs Pritchard, dressed in a salmon-coloured slip, sat, her flesh white and soft. The cat jumped onto her lap and she grimaced a smile and made a fuss over it. Pritchard brought a bowl of steaming water and set it down, and stiffly his wife put her feet into it. Her mouth was going full blast. Pritchard went around her chair and stood rubbing her neck, looking out of the window all the time.

Gwylan put her hands to Morgan's face and covered his eyes with cool fingers. 'Your room is full of ghosts,' she said.

Then he knew. 'I'm afraid of ghosts,' he answered.

They sat on the edge of the bed and, as if reassuring each

47

other, spoke softly for a while of this silly thing and that, brow against brow. A congestion in his throat eased and he listened to the sound of his heart (was it also the sound of hers?) and to the inevitable seawaves, and he was willing to let himself go, forgetting technique.

★　　★　　★　　★　　★

It was quiet. The wind, almost gone, rubbed wet hands about the house. Candle-flame figures slowly danced along the curve of the curtains. Cold-sweated brow against crisp pillows, shoulders rough-blanketrubbed. It had come and gone like soft swelling water against the ribs of a boat; round and round like a straw in the puzzles of a stream. Up and down like the squeezings of a heart . . . or the breathing of a beast.

This was as it should be—almost.

CHAPTER THREE

WHEN Morgan awoke he was alone and the day was slinking into summer, the sky high with white clouds turning over. ('The end of rain is announced by a little man with a couple of huhs and a yellow rag,' Grando used to say.) He arose and stood at the window. The previous day had been a dream but now the world had substance. Seagulls, like airborn, stillborn crabs, sailed white against the blue, black against the white. The slowing sea was brown where two valleys pursed themselves around the harbour like lips around a thumb, was green far out with flecks of white. Shadows flowed like thoughts up and over the hills. On the hillside blue smoke rose from stone cottages and white houses stood with white barns.

From the window the town was that size—framed within it. A one-smoke town that could be measured by an arm's stretch. But then nothing, he thought, is larger than what you can put your arms around: nothing makes sense without a man for size. So, at arm's length, the night-sky plough is held between the thumb and second finger, and that is its size; and when entering the gates of a castle this is unhappiness unless you can say two can enter by it—and that is its size. A woman is a wonderful size, and so is a bar door, or a blazing bush, or a plain from a mountain top, a boat from a beach. A barrel is a handy size, and a pony, and a double bass, and an apple in the hand, and a child at the knee.

Time cannot be measured in such a way—with relation to a man's size or to his age, or even to what is familiar to him . . . The time it takes to wash a shirt is not the same as the time it takes to drown a cat.

The colour of the day and the darkness of the day spoils time, makes it easier to put a tag on it. Morning or Evening, as if that explains everything. The drab cities of the south, the coal valleys, the train journey, the green valley in sun and in storm, this place, were all known in the same day. In one small part of a day, in the same dark with no light between an old man had talked out of sleep and a woman had acted from her heart. Experiences ages apart. And the night had been long. There had been deep peace and a dark joy, then the woman dressing in the still dark and leaving him. Later, in daylight, the awakening to a closing door and breakfast had been by the bed.

After eating he went back to his own room but it seemed cold and empty so he grabbed a coat and left. At the bottom of the stairs fat little Pritchard stood with lather over half his face as if frothing out of one side of his mouth.

'I would like a word, Mr Johns,' Pritchard said, waving a cut-throat razor.

'If I've got it you get it,' Morgan said. The sun was bright through the dimpled glass of the front door.

'It is like this. We are not ready for visitors just yet so we are afraid we cannot put you up any longer.'

'Is thirty shillings not enough?'

'It is not the money . . .' With a delicate finger Pritchard scratched through the lather under his chin. A mechanical squeaking sound around the passage corner but what caused it stopped out of sight.

'I'm staying in town for just a few more days,' said Morgan. 'It'd be a drag to move. I'll stretch it to two pounds a night.'

'It is not the money, as I've said.' A breathless whistle came into his voice. 'You will have to go for we are just not ready for visitors.'

'So you're not ready! That's OK. I could see that by the condition of my room. But if I don't mind why do you?'

'It is inconvenient.'

'Look man, if it's the flute bit, forget it. I don't want to blow any more anyway.'

'I cannot do it.'

'Two pounds and you needn't make the bed.' ('If you want to get at the truth, Charlie—get them angry.') 'I was assured London coin was good in the provinces. It's got the queen's head on it an' all. What's good enough for her's good enough for me. Isn't it good enough for you?'

'I tell you . . .' Pritchard was struggling now '. . . you will have to go.'

'I understand that bit, but I don't get the why of it.'

The squeaking started up again and a wheelchair turned the corner. The woman in it spoke in Welsh and Morgan turned to her. Her face was yellow and her lips were thin and tight. The time was not for greetings.

'What's wrong?' Morgan asked.

'Why ask her?' Pritchard said, suddenly excited and

51

wiping at the lather on his face with a dirty handkerchief. 'I just told you that we cannot put you up any more. Plain as plain I said it.'

'Careful, man—you'll wet your reed.'

'Having difficulty understanding me you are and me speaking plain English but two words in a row from you are foreign.' Pritchard walked around in a circle and rubbed his hands over his face: half his face rasped with gooseberry bristles.

'What you leaking about?'

'Leaking? Leaking? Do you see a puddle?' said Pritchard.

'What's under your shirt?'

'Nothing is under there. Only me. But forgetting you are that this is a respectable public house. We do not have to take people.'

'Is that the way to do business?'

'It is not a business we have here I would like you to know, but an establishment. We take whom we please.'

Morgan laughed. 'All right. Is there another establishment in this town?'

'And do not laugh at me if you please. You come in here, wander around my place at night, never in your room, put us to trouble. Supper you want, fire you want, and what else I do not know.'

Morgan tapped him on the chest with two stiff fingers. 'You're getting paid.'

'Not yet I have.'

A squealing of the wheelchair accompanied Mrs Pritchard's voice and a breathing hard came through Pritchard's. Both speaking at once.

'Stand in line there,' said Morgan, but the noise increased.

'Take your things into the street now,' said pink Pritchard, and the high wailing of his wife seemed to express the same sentiments.

'I'll be out by noon,' said Morgan.

'I need the room,' said Pritchard.

Then Morgan saw Gwylan leaning against the wall behind Mrs Pritchard. She was smiling and he stopped his reply to return it. In the calm, Pritchard tried to move his belly up into his chest.

'Why don't you leave your things in my room until you find another place,' Gwylan said. Mrs Pritchard spun around and wheeled away talking a furious Welsh to herself.

'You have no shame,' the publican said.

'No shame have you,' she answered. 'A man comes all this way to visit and into the street you throw him.'

'I have explained . . .'

'Thanks,' Morgan said to her. Then to Pritchard, 'I'll creep out of the crypt by noon.' At the door he turned. 'You've got lather up your nose,' he said.

Outside the day was bright around him.

The air was thick with the fecundity of the earth: the sky was like a cave for the song of birds. Seeds-or-something, heavy with moisture, plopped from the trees, and creatures in the branches chattered.

Small silver moths fluttered up from the foliage, tantalizing the *Unicorn* cat. It jumped at one and missed, landing in a puddle, and ran off, stopping every other step to shake its paws. With the cat gone a bird went back to its tap-tapping at a snail.

Flower stalks had been snapped in the night, bushes had been uprooted, and here and there the trees were whitened by broken limbs. The road was decked with blown leaves and the roadside ditches ran full with muddy water.

Down in the hollow of the one street, away from the *Unicorn* and away from the cross roads which opened the village face to the harbour and the hills, the shops were opening.

A man with staring eyes below a bulging brow, and all his ample body slipping below a concave chest, arranged in his sleep a washboard and a bath outside his ironmonger's shop, not looking with his all-seeing eyes. As Morgan passed he turned to watch. A greyhaired woman, shapeless as a carelessly peeled potato, came out to look on the pretext of picking over her apples and Brussels sprouts. The milkman, his face a bursting of vein endings, seemed embarrassed at the greeting he gave, and he shook the bell reins to make the dainty horse move on. An old woman on her knees struggled to get up from the white-stone rubbing of the white-stone step.

Morgan stopped to scratch a big, black-balled Siamese cat sitting on a window ledge, and saw an old frightened face squeezed by pulled lace. An errand boy, slanting his buttocks as he reached for the pedals, snaked past and shouted, 'Watcha mate.'

'Watcha,' Morgan shouted back.

Women, talking near the red-pillar-boxed store, called to their curious children, and two middle-aged dead-eyed biddies bent their heads and exchanged suspicions as he passed. A pub—the *Rose and Crown*—too small, perhaps, for rooms, was quiet with the blinds down.

At the crossroads Morgan turned and crossed the bridge and walked along the quay around the harbour, trailing his feet across the sea marks and seaweed and tar strips. He passed a dropping of houses, pink-washed, sunk with dormers resting on the sand: farther on, where the sea had

54

been, sat a shell of a house. Where the arm of the quay started to reach back towards the town a cottage with grass on its roof stood with a row of tarred huts, their backs to the surf. The sea met the land with a scalloped edge, and when the waves fell back they took rattling pebbles with them. Nudging boats were afloat in river water and rotting boats were resting with their shoulders in the tide-out mud.

From the dark of the last shed sang a hymn-tuned baritone . . .

> Guide me, O Thou great Jehovah
> For I fear I cannot stand.
> The beer was bad or else the brandy,
> Hold me with Thy powerful hand.
> Bread of heaven,
> Bread of heaven,
> Feed me till I want no more . . . want no more . . .
> Feed me till I want no more.

Inside the shed was a rowboat, upturned, and tarpaulins and nets were draped from the rafters. The man who sang went on to the next verse. Morgan flicked away his cigarette and waited for it to end. Suddenly the singer jumped.

'Christ Almighty—a visitation!' He clasped his hands to his chest and glared with one blue eye as its glass mate pointed to the sky. (Maybe in the country of the one-eyed, the man with a good nose is king.) 'Palpitations! Do you always creep up on a man like that?'

'I coughed.'

'Coughed! I thought it was the creaking of the gates of hell. Indeed to God. There I was blaspheming nineteen to the half-dozen and you appearing like an avenging angel.

The flaming sun at your back and all. If you'd said "Peter sent me" I'd have dropped a load there and then.'

'There's no wings on me.'

'Glad I am to see it.' He crossed himself, chanting, 'Ace, king, queen, jack.'

William Williams was fat with sun-white hair and eyebrows, and a great nose in blossom. Shredded dungarees were rolled to his hairy calves and dirty white slops were on his feet. A thick sweater unravelled at the neck and waist.

'I heard all about you,' he said. 'Come looking for a man named Rhydderch isn't it?'

'Do you know him?'

Will Twice tapped himself all over. 'Have you got a fag?' Morgan offered the pack and he took one for his mouth and one for behind his ear. A couple of puffs, then he took the cigarette out of his mouth, smelled the end, then tapped it with his thumb. 'What's this?'

'A filter.'

'Oh aye.' He puffed some more. 'Like drinking wine through a cork.'

'Can never please you people. Give you imports and you bitch; give you your own make and you wonder.'

'What you expect. We poor bastards always worry what the blessed are keeping from us.' After another drag he said, 'Rhydderch. I never heard of him.' He went into the dark of the shed again and came out with a cane lobster pot, a coil of wire, and a green flagon of beer. 'There is no man here with that name.' With a pull at his tight crotch he sat down on the quay, his legs against the slimed seaweed and his feet just above the water. Morgan sat next to him.

56

'Have you lived here long?'

'A couple of bloody lives, off and on.' He shook his head. 'There's a place to come. Dyfnaint's dead like the buried. Perhaps it's the wrong place you got off at.'

'I followed a lead,' Morgan said.

'Rich you must be eh?—wandering around.'

'No.'

'Have a drop.'

Morgan tilted the bottle, looking through it at the sun. One mouth-filling gulp of cool beer, flat and bitter.

'Notice how some people wipe their hands across the mouth of a bottle if you offer it,' Will said. 'Afraid they might catch something from your gob. They're the kind who stand on lavatory seats.'

'It's good beer.'

Will Twice drank, his cornered Adam's apple lifting and falling, his eyes closed. When he had finished, he opened his trousers and fished out his penis; holding it like an egg, he directed a yellow stream into the water.

'That is what turns the sea to salt,' he said.

The tide-out had stopped, and, about to come in, was pushing against the river flow. A boy waved from across the harbour and Will waved back. The boy sat on the wharf and took off his shoes, then tied them by their strings and hung them around his neck. With feet turned out he ran down the stone steps, and with feet turned in, across the sand, flicking toe drops as he ran.

Will, winding wire round the splitting cane of the lobster pot, said, 'Winter's gone for good, for good.'

'I must go too,' Morgan said.

'Lived in the city too long you have boyo. No one here has to do anything they do not want to do.'

'I've got to find a place to stay. I've been kicked out of the *Unicorn*.'

'Aye? There's strange for you, for they are both fond of pennies. You been messing about with my daughter?'

'There was nothing messy, though we met.'

'That's it,' said Will. 'Abso–bloody–lutely! For a fat old man Pritchard's got a couple of hot clangers, and as his wife will not or can not any more, he's been after Gwylan. Not a chance he's got but—sure, he saw a glimmer in your eye and took precautions.'

'That might be it.'

'I bet the wind blew, etcetera.'

'There was a breeze.'

'Pritchard's all right,' said Will. 'See you—there is nothing wrong with his old woman.'

'She's no cripple?'

'Not any more.' The boy had stopped running half-way across the harbour and was now looking at Morgan, his eyes serious. Then not looking he came slowly, dragging his toes. 'A proper martyr she likes to be,' went on Will, 'keeping him close with her crying. She chronstantly suffers, she says. After living with her for twenty years his idea of hell is being tempted by a nice, plump woman with no snatch. D'you know the only thing that would save old Pritchard now?'

'What?'

'It is a glass eye like my lefty. She hates it. I've worked out a whole jig of tricks to jangle her nerves so bad she can't keep her bum still. When she's keeping bar alone I order a bottle of stout and after my first swig, I say—always the same, like a ritual—I say, "Good stuff that. It's enough to petrify the eyeballs," and I taps it with the mouth of the bottle. Oh she doesn't like that. Another thing I do is close my good eye and open wide the stiff one so the glass stare is right at her. But my best is—what you think?'

'I don't know.'

'I pops out my glass ollie and I sucks it.' He choked over his laughter, his good eye rolling.

'What's it taste like?'

'Like a periwinkle.'

'You and your brother ought to go there together,' Morgan said.

'Caradoc won't wear his glass eye—says he can't see through it.'

'How'd you both lose them?' Morgan asked.

'Aye, they all ask. What are the possibilities then? Chemistry, assault, accident, disease. He by one, I by another, I usually say. He on a hawthorn, I when a whore spat through a keyhole. It is easier believing that . . . It was fish-hooks. Identically. That's all I've ever caught, Caradoc says. Together I say we can see as well as the best; he says it is needed to shut one eye to each other's faults.' He offered the bottle. 'Pritchard's all right. We will go back one of these nights and drink free from him.' Then, pointing at the scratch, he said, 'Did my daughter do that?'

'Nothing but a tender hand from her.'

'Aye, women are seldom unpredictable in a storm.'

'It's trees you can't trust,' said Morgan.

'The sea is the only safe place to be.' His Adam's apple up-and-downed again.

'D'you know of a bed?' Morgan asked.

'Is it a room you want? There are no empty houses in Dyfnaint.'

'Anything. I won't be staying long.'

59

'See the house above the trees on the side of the hill?' Will said. 'How'd you like to stay there?'

The house was shabby with a sagging roof but it looked across the valley to the south and out to sea; behind it a path went up and over the hill to the hills beyond.

'It's close enough for comfort but not really a part of the village,' Will said.

'Suits me.'

The boy had stopped at the river's edge. 'Early you are, Owen,' Will said to him. 'I am not ready yet.'

'Why not?' asked the boy, his tongue sticking out through a two-tooth gap as if in rudeness.

'Go back to your house and ask your Mam if she will rent her room to this fellow.'

'I just came from there.'

'It is nice you are getting exercise then.'

'How long is he going to stay?' asked the boy.

'You just go and ask, that's all,' said Will. 'You are the agent not the bloody manager.'

'The tide is moving fast,' said the boy.

'The sooner you get back the sooner we can go.'

Sullen, the boy walked a few paces, then turned. 'Willie,' he shouted, his hands thrust deep into his pockets. 'She'll be mad. She's busy and doesn't want anyone.'

'Ask anyway.'

The boy spat into the mud, and with head down shuffled sand over the spit. Then he turned and slouched away.

'No use it is sending a boy on a journey with a purpose,' said Will. 'Every step he takes gives him a reason for doing something else. If we weren't going fishing he would be gone all day.'

The boy jumped a rope which sagged from a tilted boat,

tipping it so that he sprawled onto his knees. He got up, walked a few steps and quickly turned and jumped again. He cleared it and gave a prolonged cheer, shaking his clenched fists above his head. A few shadow-boxing steps, a running kick at a clump of seaweed then a run with flailing arms and he was at a redrusty ladder, and up he went scorning the stone steps. A little girl with long hair pale in the sun stood watching from the wharf so he waited awhile dangling from a rung with a taut arm.

'Why isn't he in school?' Morgan asked.

'God knows. He's never lost for a reason—Queen's birthday, the teacher's sick, Good Friday (coming on a Tuesday).' He went into the shed and came out with another bottle which he offered.

'It is good going to sea with a boy,' he said. 'A boy is afraid of nothing.'

'He's afraid of me.'

'Well then, a boy is not afraid of much.'

'Why is he afraid of me?'

'Perhaps because you are a boy no more.'

'He's not afraid of you.'

'Perhaps he thinks a boy it is I am.'

The boy still waited with the little girl on the cobblestones across the harbour. He waved his arms and dodged about as if grappling with something.

'Shoo!' Will suddenly shouted, waving at seagulls. 'Stop pooping all over my clean boat.'

The girl shook her head and the boy nodded his, then she stuck out her tongue and moved away. The boy hopped on one leg, laughing out some taunts, then ran on behind the houses, later appearing on the path leading to the trees on the side of the hill.

'What would you do?' asked Will. 'Suppose it is ship-
wrecked you are and all alone in a small boat and rough it
is and dark. All one night and all the day that follows and
towards night again you wake up from a doze and you see,
coming up from out the sea behind your boat, two arms
waving as if in sleep. And one hand grasps the stern. What
would you do?'

'I'd flip.'

'I lifted the oar and smashed it down on the hand with all
my strength and then when the hand was gone I smashed
the oar again where the hand had been. That hand felt real
it did when I hit it but now I do not know. I asked the boy
what he would do if it happened to him and he said help
him out, and I said help who out, and he said help him who
wanted to get into the boat. So I said do you think he was
real, and he said what do you mean, and I said what if he
was not a real man, and he answered perhaps it was a man
from the sea and needed help because he did not have legs
and maybe he had a message. What kind of message I then
said and the boy said where the land was.' He drank, then,
ignoring the cigarette behind his ear, said, 'Got a fag?'

Morgan, watching the trees, held out the pack and said,
'Keep them.' Soon the boy came out of the woods at the
same place he had entered, and came back down the hill
with no dallying. As he ran down the steps and towards
them, Will said, 'Mrs Parry'll be as pleased as a hen with a
cackling fart to get your money but she won't be pleased
with you. She's just like my old lady was.'

'You sound glad to be solo.'

'Aye. Fifteen years with her was a long, long time.
Vanity got her in the end, thank God. She had her ears
pierced and they got infected. I never did like her.'

The boy stopped at the river and said, 'Let's go fishing.'

'What did your Mam say?' Will asked.

Owen looked up at a seagull and followed its sailing. 'She said she can't now because she isn't ready and it isn't summer yet. So he can't come.'

Will whispered, 'The little bastard didn't go.'

Morgan said to Owen, 'Thanks anyway.'

Will whispered on, 'All that time doing the dog with all his phantoms and he couldn't spare five minutes to climb the hill.'

The boy's eyes were wide and blue. Absently he bent and picked a pebble from between his toes. 'She says he cannot come because she is spring-cleaning and there is a bird's nest down the chimney in the spare room.'

'What else did she say, Owen boy?' Will said, laughing.

'Nothing.'

'You did not take long.'

'I ran.' The boy rolled his short trousers and stepped into the river. 'I'm going to come across this way.'

'You will be swept out to sea and be eaten by lobsters and shrimps.'

'It is not very deep.'

'Come on then.'

'But it is terribly fast.'

'Well go around then.'

Owen took his shoes from around his neck and threw them across the river onto the quay. A step and the water was to his knees and it stayed there until he was almost across when it dipped to his thighs.

'Cold it is,' he said.

He hunched up his shoulders as if pulling himself out of the water, then rolled his short trousers even higher. The sun edged behind a cloud, and the water, swirling about his legs, turned dark and turned over bringing up sunken straws. The boy tried to find a steady rock on the river bottom and when he thought he had found it he took a step but with his eyes on Morgan and he stumbled. He fell forward onto the piled rocks against the quay with his hands holding and the river tugging at him. Will just sat watching. Morgan jumped down, reached out and gave Owen his hand and held him with a strong grip.

'Wet you are,' Willie Twice said, and laughed. The others laughed too. The boy ran into the shed, his laughter echoing.

'Walk back around and cross the bridge,' Will said to Morgan, 'and you go up the hill again. From there you can see our cockeyed world.' When Morgan turned to go Will added, 'When you come next time bring some beer.'

*   *   *   *   *

At the end of the path a gate lay on its side and behind it stood a square, sagging farmhouse with a ball of snot at each windowed nostril. Patches of whitewash lay like dandruff. The door gaped and smoke seeped from a cracked chimney. A paint-peeling barn was encircled by dilapidated buildings with roofs askew and holed roofs and no roofs. The yard shelved into a hollow with flood water. A straight tree stood looking at itself and a wizened tree leaned into the water with black hands out to stop its fall. Below, the valley stretched like an arm's mark in wet sand.

Two dogs, one nearly a collie, came timid but barking— twofaced dogs with wagging tails—and two defiantly afraid cats watched from a woodpile. A grindstone sodden in its well of slush from leaves and droppings and insect mould.

64

A rusty pump in a splash of water, scuffed ground now muddied.

Morgan stood before the open door with the dogs waiting. His knock echoed in a silent house. A girl, almost a woman, stood on the hilltop looking down at him. The small wind pressed her dress against her and then about her in swirls; her legs, astride, were long, her chest with only a hint of bosom. Her hair was the colour of autumn gorse.

Morgan turned to the wind, and a bird sang. Then it was he felt he wanted to stay awhile above the world he fancied he once knew.

Footsteps came from the house and he turned to an old, middle-aged woman. Her eyes were bulged out by thick glasses and her face was twisted into a self-conscious smile.

'Ho then, good morning,' she said. Her jowls wobbled.

'Good morning. I'm looking for a room. I was told you sometimes rent.'

'Well I have in the past—yes but—' she looked wildly about. 'It isn't the time of year at all.'

Morgan looked up at the sun. 'It's getting to be,' he said.

'Wait a minute then,' she said.

As Morgan waited he watched the girl come down the hill. The dogs were greeting her when the whispers in the house stopped and footsteps returned.

Now there were two of them. The man said, 'You want a room?' His mouth was small and his voice high but his body was like a barrel. His puffy eyelids drooped over his blue eyes.

'Yes.'

'For how long?'

'A couple of days.'

'It wouldn't pay just for a few days.' His lower lip was

split and wet and he tried not to use it when speaking. 'Will you guarantee a week?'

'You know . . .' giggled the woman with a nervous nose-nudging of her glasses.

'I guess I can,' said Morgan.

'Four pounds a week it will be,' said the man.

'Includes breakfast it does,' said the woman.

'I'd like to see the room,' Morgan said, and the man turned away.

The woman said, 'This is Mair, our daughter.' The girl from the hill came up and, not smiling, said hello, quietly. Her pale skin showed the coursing of blue veins under her eyes. 'And I am Mrs Parry,' the woman added.

After the introductions she led the way into the house, which, unlike the yard, was orderly. The floor was stone and there were heavy beams and a wood stove. They climbed ladder-like stairs.

'This is the hired men's room,' she said. 'You will have to go through it to reach your room, but quiet they are.'

The room was small with dark wood and a leaded window. On the window sill were two brass candlesticks with white candlestumps. The curtains were red and the quilt was of many colours. From the window Morgan could see the *Unicorn*, the river twisting like a serpent along the valley, and the sea beyond.

'I'll take it,' he said.

CHAPTER FOUR

THE WIND took her hair and held it up and twined it around her throat, and the sun turned it silver. Almost like a creature that must be observed out of the corner of the eye, or with the aid of a mirror, she turned away and went over the hill when she saw that he was watching her. Morgan left the Parrys' yard and took what seemed to be a short cut across the fields in the direction of the village. He walked slowly, reluctantly enjoying the day.

The trouble with some days, he thought, is that you can see too far, too clearly. It is as if the earth falls away and becomes refined and then is pulled back through an unblemished glass so that the colour in the bottom of the furrow half a valley away is distinct from the colour of the soil turned over. Every aspect of the world is there, all the deformities, every perfection; all sins, all glories, all accidents, all errors . . . each conformity.

So much clarity that it is like unreality. It is as if all things that should be there, have been emptied, just this minute, from the scene. Yet there are eyes all over. What is that line of trees and hedges for if not to hide something behind. If a man stopped to crouch over a beetle on a rock, everything within the whole horizon would wait and watch until he straightened up and moved on.

Morgan picked up a stone and threw it towards the line of trees. He heard it fall but he scared up nothing: the trees were farther than he thought. The clouds seemed high and the curve of the coast distant. All the mountains were there as in a child's drawing, one peak appearing behind the other, the farthest range hardly dimmer than the first.

Morgan could not remember when last he had been alone. As a child he had been alone, ('Let me stay until there are three more stars'—sleepy but desperate at the intrusion, trying to grasp back at the peace. Of course it was gone and the three more stars were already out there.) but a child chooses to be alone. (Chanting to the solitary game of dribbling sand through the fingers; there was something hypnotic about it and soon the empty world was populated.)

He walked on in silence, wanting noise . . . Yet there was no silence here. Merely an absence of noises that were familiar. There were all sorts of chatterings and whistlings and whisperings together. They were not watching, these creatures in the trees and hedges. They were as unconcerned of him as he had been of them. As he had been of people in a town's crowd; as he had been of towns and trees and fruit stands and railroad depots along the way from one place to another. Even between cities, in the past, there had been only so many hours. Not even miles. Yet there's always something a man's not unconcerned about. At this time, back there, there'd be thick coffee and elbows on the table with an hour-long morning paper. There'd be things to talk about. Here the grass was long and the birds were singing but on the sea no ships were coming or going.

He passed through the field and crossed the stile and saw the chapel he had passed the night before. In the daytime it looked shabby, no longer sinister. It was of grey stone with red brick around the windows, and SALEM CHAPEL was in black over the door. On a notice board with the hours o the services was a quotation—THE MEEK SHALL INHERIT THE EARTH. The day became quiet and frozen as if just this moment entranced . . . but it passed. Morgan climbed over a low stone wall and into the graveyard which spread along the hill.

White marble maidens with modest thighs and boyish chests bowed their heads over wax flowers in inverted glass bowls. There were grassy mounds with no headstones, tilted slate slabs with lichen-filled carvings, sturdy stone boxes within iron railings tall enough to keep out soulsnatchers. No newly dug graves.

He read the inscriptions. Bleddyn Vaughan, Idwal and Ceridwen Owens, Glyndwr ap Owen Richards, John William Llewellyn, David Jones, Maggie Lewis. No melting pot here. There was a Rhydderch but dead since 1812. Morgan knelt and felt the worn letters on the stone . . .

HE

LIVED

ALONE,

SADLY

CLAIMING

HAPPINESS

A mist rose from the soft ground, and the cobwebbed grasses held tears of rain. There was the look of neglect and the smell of decay.

Morgan stood up and turned to go and saw a face at a

window. It disappeared, and although he waited, no one came out. He tried the heavy chapel door but it was locked and when he shook it the clanging echoed. He walked around to the living quarters at the rear and knocked there but had no answer. He bent down and put his eye to the keyhole but the key was in it: he placed his ear against the door but no sound came through it. In the quiet was heard only a soft rustling in the grasses, and the distant call of crows.

The gate, sunk in tall nettles, squealed as he passed through it to the road, along which he went, his footsteps for company.

The *Unicorn* was near, and the time was noon. His visit was brief. Gwylan was not about but his bag was packed. He saw an awkward but polite Pritchard, paid him, picked up the stationmaster's lantern and left. But before he left the grounds he walked to the sea side of the inn and noted the position of the window which would be lighted to await the taptap of pebbles.

The day was drying out. The dripping from the bushes had ceased, and the moths had found another bed. The cat from the *Unicorn* watched the birds with their punctured snails and occasionally made a stalking movement, but only out of defeat.

As Morgan neared the chapel again he saw the door open and a tall man in a dark suit appear and lean over the wall to blow a noseful into the graveyard before withdrawing into the chapel. Morgan hurried, and went through the gate and up to the door. He knocked and opened it without waiting.

Tall in the pulpit with his arms outstretched towards the psalm board, the preacher looked like a frightened prophet.

Dark-eyed and pale, his cheeks sucked in, his hair sticking up like bullrushes, he dropped his hands to the pulpit rim and tightened the wrinkles in his brow.

'Am I butting in?' Morgan asked.

'I thought perhaps, sir, you had come to sing a song to God.' His melancholy voice came through a stuffed nose.

Morgan looked about him. The last place to sing a song! The chapel, dark in the light which filtered through the green and violet windows, looked like the belly of a boat. It had a dozen ribs of high-backed benches, and heavy wooden arches above. There was a smell of wax and old tapestry and lavender and mothballs and dead flowers: of many things but not of soap and sunshine.

The preacher sneezed twice, held a large handkerchief to his face and blew a loud rasp, then hurriedly stuffed it away as if ashamed of it. 'I see you all the time, sir,' he said in a voice half-way between accusation and apology.

'Destiny, maybe.' But it was the wrong line. The preacher closed the door of the pulpit, resisting, and stood like a stone saint. 'I thought perhaps you'd know most of the people who've lived here in your time. There is a man I'm trying to find though he may now be dead.'

'The Lord have mercy on his soul.'

'Do you remember a man who came here a long time . . .'

'Beyond the power of memory, sir.' The voice sang up and down but with no expression.

'It wasn't that long.'

'The Lord does not permit one to dwell upon the long past. It is so written. Only the sins of the world. Glad I am to know. What is past is past. Holy, holy, holy.'

Morgan grunted.

'Fear God above all else and let all other things be. Do not disturb. Do not intrude.'

Morgan breathed on the beak of the brass bird which held the book and passed his sleeve over it. 'Don't you want to know his name—the man I'm looking for.'

'One name only we need; one way only to look. I do not know your man, but let me tell you of my master.'

'I'll tell you mine if you tell me yours,' said Morgan, smiling.

'Come to chapel Sunday.' It was a plea. 'I am preaching on the way of the wicked. English you must be so come and hear good preaching and good singing.'

'D'you ever preach on the ways of the wise?'

'The ways of the world. The world is wicked.' He came out of the pulpit and carefully came down the steps. As he did so he seemed to shrink. He sat in the front pew, one hand grasping the sweat-blackened wood, and wiped at his eyes with his large handkerchief.

'I try,' he said. 'I speak the word of the Lord. I cry Hosanna in the highest. Repent I say. I say the Lord will strike you down dead.' He shook his head and blew his nose. 'They worship everything but the Lord God.' He brought out a book from his pocket. 'The word of the Lord is written,' he went on, holding the book above his head. 'Everything is here. A guide, a signpost, a warning, a reward. Never stray from it.'

'No doubt about it,' Morgan said, going to the door.

'Come on Sunday,' the preacher called.

'Sure,' he answered, thinking, 'I'll be gone like the winter, be gone, be gone.'

★   ★   ★   ★   ★

The branches from a six-foot section of the fallen tree had been chopped away and the stationmaster was sawing at the trunk. When he saw Morgan he stopped but gave no greeting. Morgan swung his arm to show the lantern then put the lantern down with his bag.

'Have you got a second handle for the saw?' Morgan asked.

The old man nodded and, as Morgan took off his coat, he got the handle from his coat and screwed it in the other end. Morgan gripped the saw and braced his foot against the trunk. With a nod at each other they began sawing. Morgan was unpractised and sometimes he buckled the saw but the old man made no comment. Steadily they worked and Morgan was blowing hard before they had finished the first cut. He stuck it until they cut through but when the stationmaster moved the saw immediately to a new cut, he held up his hand and grinned.

'I'll give you a rest, Caradoc,' he said, adding, 'Gwylan gave me your name.'

'And she came and gave me yours,' he answered with only a hint of a smile. He was breathing easily though his brow was spotted with sweat. His new-shaven skin shone smooth and tight. 'You remind me of someone I loved long ago, Morgan. You have a coalminer's face. It suggests religion and poetry and a stubbornness. I see a mourning in it.'

'Yours is the face that's mournful.'

'I am too old,' Caradoc said. 'I daydream. Things happen and I say to myself because of it this too must surely happen. This and this and this. Before I know it fancy becomes fact, then if up comes fact when I want fancy—then I am sad.'

'I'm stiff on dreams. I just worry.'

'I will never remember until it is too late that nothing is ever as one says it is. It is only like.' He shook his head. 'A good listener you are, Morgan. Last night you flattered an old man. You listened while I turned over old pictures and then you showed me new ones. And when you had gone I could not sleep. I could hear my heart like horses in the snow . . . It seems that there are two worlds separated by a wide sea, where there is no understanding. One land sings with the tenor voice of legend; its mountains submit to the sky. The known thing—that the world does not change—is spoken to a new child so that his feet are not lost in a place not known. There is movement in the grasses and in the water and in the white clouds. Beyond that there is no prediction . . . From the other land the stars are unfamiliar as if seen from the dark side, and I feel that until they can be reached they are considered of no value. The dead, I gather, are but one deep and a limb to an acre. The earth has not been turned, yet the rivers have changed since dawn, the skyline since noon. And a man with creation in his grasp has nothing to say to his neighbours . . . The pictures were not at all the same. I said to myself this man who has crossed the seas will stay awhile, and let me look at him. I am sorry to see you ready to leave.'

Morgan, pleased, said, 'If you see a man with a brick it doesn't mean he's going to throw it. Or a man with an egg—doesn't mean he's going to hatch it.' He kicked his bag. 'This isn't going anyplace—except to the Parrys'. I've got a room there for a week. And maybe I'll stay that long.'

Caradoc bent to the saw again. 'Glad I am,' he said.

They worked without stopping until they were through

the trunk, then they took two of the chopped branches and levered the section away from the path. Caradoc picked up the lantern and shouldered the saw.

'Stay for leek and kidney pie,' he said. 'Gwylan made it.'

CHAPTER FIVE

THE PLACE was like a church: a vaulted fireplace, the flames an altar, the counter a pulpit from which Maggie called and got a prayerful response, the colours in a window were bottles on a shelf, the big book was the slate on the wall. The spittoons were the nearest thing to a plate. No cold straight seats but chairs with arms, no creaking narrow board for the knees but a bar of brass for the foot. The rain-water voices of children and the uncertain voices of lordly ladies were missing—and no one missed them. Smoke, smell, male murmur: this was the *Rose and Crown*, no church. Hymns had been played but no god was invoked. Praise was due in the earth-turning day while walking behind a head-down horse; praise was due on the turning sea, casting onto grey water. Praise was given alone, joy in company.

The men, stiff booted, tight trousered . . .

'Maggie, oh Maggie.' William Williams, one arm reaching down over his shoulder, backed through the gap in the counter until he came up against the sink. 'Scratch my back, Maggie.'

While pulling at the beer pump with one hand she slipped the other under his sweater.

'There, there—oh there, love,' said Will. 'Now lower. It's moving.'

'I am not going to stand here all night following your itch all over,' said Maggie. 'It is a bath you need.'

'Give me one for my birthday,' he said.

The men, stiff booted, tight trousered, were not unlike each other (What's left of love after two hills and a river on a rainy night. Love must be found nearby). Stubby they were like cigar butts. All with the same hard brown skin, black hair, and often the weird blue eyes, but the home-made haircuts and the different whisker shapes showed no compulsion to look alike. Faces were serious, moving into laughter only when amusement could not be contained.

Farmers and fishermen had come first; farmers would leave first, fishermen last. Farmers not taking off their heavy coats, standing facing the fire; fishermen at home with their backsides to the heat. All, standing or sitting, with tankards held with the hand through the handle, scorning it, hand-clasped around the body of the pint—hands that were like the bark of a tree, fingers thick and clumsy with flat, blackened nails.

The voices . . .

'. . . always sounded like a chicken did Maggie's husband,' Will was saying. 'In his marriage he wanted to be able to say everything in the garden was lovely, and it was a vege-table garden at that. Not too keen to squeeze the pump-kin. A sailor he was—is maybe for all we know. Hasn't been home for eight years, and me and Maggie are glad of it.'

The voices, nicely tuned, had a melodic line ungoverned by meaning but with an unvarying rhythm. The talk came with the pleasure of babel after a lonely day. Words, in Welsh or English, sounded as if they were the seldom used communication, and hands were needed often. Maggie's hands were busy and her voice rang out like a chorister's as she sang back, 'Bulldog, half a bitter, black and tan, a couple of milds, mother's ruin . . .'

Maggie was pink and fat . . .

'. . . and isn't it a joyful way she has of pulling a pint. Look how graceful her arm is. There is a kind of urgency in it. Oh she warms my cockles. Maggie,' Will called. 'Tell the man why they call me Willy-two-times.'

'Because his name is William Williams, sir.'

'Come now, Maggie, that is not the only reason.'

'I am sure that I do not know what else it could be,' she said, turning her back.

Maggie was pink and fat with a broad bum; her laughter was like a rolling ball with bells inside. Her hair was long but untidy, and her moustache was golden. In a moment's calm she bent, hand to her hair, to a Gold Flake mirror in front of which was a bunch of bluebells in a bowl: seen as reflected in a pool she was a wild creature in a bluebell wood.

. . . 'Oh Maggie, don't you read, don't you know,' Morgan sang to himself. The younger Maggie too was wild . . .

t'rum–t'rum

> I knew a Maggie, Maggie
>> and I knew her mother too–oo.
> She was pretty as an angel
>> —and so was Maggie too–oo.

t'rum–t'rum

> One was black as black could be
>> and one was yeller, yell–er.
> Black Ma she was too old for me
>> —but I could not, would not tell her.

t'rum–t'rum

> I wanted for to marry her
>> but her daughter wasn't will–ing.
> And so I married Maggie–love
>> —and got eighteen pennies for a shill–ing.

t'rum–t'rum

> Her Ma she loved me pow'fully
>> 'twas useless to resist her.
> But then she brought another wench
>> —and called her younger sister.

t'rum–t'rum

> Black Ma she wore a yellow robe
>> (her daughter wore a red one).
> When Maggie cut her, cut her up,
>> the yellow oh to red ran.

t'rum–t'rum

> 'Little Maggie, Maggie–love,
>> what shall we, shall we, do–oo?'
> 'Hold me, hold me, Charlie–love,
>> kiss me Charlie do–oo.'

t'rum–t'rum.

Yes, never again the scene. Sometimes Maggie but never again Black Ma . . .

Before Will and Morgan on the bar were black rums and dark stouts—a sip of one and a mouthful of the other.

Behind them the bell tinkled and the door opened, then the sand-sprinkled floor crunched as the newcomer came to the bar.

'Hello Dai Em-Em,' Will shouted to the man who had just entered. The man answered with a scowl and some muttered Welsh. Will turned to Morgan. 'Dai Em-Em—got his Military Medal in the war when they shot off both his jewels. Came back a hero but mad he was because his voice went up, so he turned Welsh Nationalist. Wants Wales for the Welsh—who else wants it I do not know. And the stupid man swears he cannot now understand a word of the English language. Myself I know he is a bloody liar as well as a bloody fool. Look at him now turning pink and me smiling pleasant as you please at him, and him knowing every word I say before him and I knowing he knows it, but him too proud to take offence. Wales for the Welsh! Next it will be South Wales for the South Walians, then Cardiganshire for the Cardies, then Dyfnaint for the Daft. A bigger land we want you dip, not a smaller.'

The man, crimson, moved on.

'Devil he calls me,' said Will. 'Sometimes I wish I were. I'd shake them up. And I'd get their souls cheap for I know them well. Only those who don't give a damn escape damnation—isn't that it? Even my brother agreed there—after a lot of thought. Go as the day goes, that's my motto . . . There is another idiot I like to talk at. Another Dai. Hello Dai Deaf, you ugly old bugger.' Dai Deaf smiled back. 'Look at that expression. Is that a smile or the sign of the passing of wind . . .'

'Maggie, give me one of your meat pies,' Morgan said.

'I wouldn't,' Will said.

'Why not?'

'Never again will I eat one of those pies. Maggie's sister makes them. I think she puts saltpetre in them.' He bent forward and whispered. 'I had an experience once after eating one of those pies. There I was all set to go with that lovely feeling like excitement when—well, I tell you—it was a spot to be in. Like having your bunting out and a flag to wave and the procession is next week.' He took the pie from Morgan's hand and turned to a man ordering at the bar. 'Jenkin, as Sanitary Inspector, what is your official opinion. Is this pie fit to eat or is it not?'

Jenkin considered the pie, weighed it in his hand. 'I have my doubts,' he said, then offered the pie to the man on his left. 'Would you examine this pie when you have time, Lloyd? This man was going to eat it, of all things.'

He picked up his beer and went back to his table. Lloyd passed the pie onto his neighbour.

'Saved you untold embarrassment,' said Will.

Around the piano were younger people standing apart, the men like young trees, the young women brazen with lipstick and white-dusted faces. Men with beer, women with port. Men like boys drinking deep; women as girls swirling the red wine and smiling at the ruby shadowed in their palms. They had started out with teasing and with laughter, had drawn closer together and had fallen into song. The piano gave out only chords. They started, softly, with a song like sea bells, like wind harps, moved on to one with the near joy of a brook, then, without a break, a change. There were songs of twilight, of moonlight, songs of countries with castles where the little hills are called mountains. Dreams of nobility but no sound of revelry or dance, and the songs of love were for someone seen but out of reach—the love for a ghost or an imprisoned maiden or for the naiad who, with the day, goes back to the lake.

The singers stopped and drained their glasses. A young man with red cheeks gathered the empty glasses from the piano top and brought them to the bar.

'Iorwerth,' Will called to him. 'Come and meet a friend of mine from America.'

'America! America!' said the boy. 'There is such a place? Not fairyland is it? Actually here is a man from America? Call us quaint, Mr Johns.'

Morgan looked him over. 'You're quaint,' he said.

'You cocky young sparrow,' said Will.

'Motorcars and motorpeople,' Iorwerth went on. 'Go like hell, I'm told, all day long. America! Where the eyes are to the top of the heap and the nose is to the wheel.'

'That's the shoulder, man,' said Morgan. 'The nose is in someone else's business—smelling out their trouble.'

'Same again, Maggie,' Iorwerth called, then to Morgan with a grin, 'Welcome to Wales.' His hand was firm.

'You are a bloody young pullet,' said Will. 'One day you will get yourself in a deep pot with a lid on it. Mark my words.'

'Words, words, Will. You've got a glass eye, a wooden head and a mouth like a tin box.'

'After my daughter you will be, as soon as you get hair around your whingding so watch your language.'

'Come to find a man you have, Mr Johns, isn't it?'

82

Iorwerth said. 'Alive or dead is he then? As much alive in the ground as up in the hills minding sheep. If any man will do, glad I would be to go with you.'

'You go to America!' Will laughed. 'Never, boy. You know why? You might be happy there, that's why. And you wouldn't be Welsh any more. Cut off you'd be from your blue-painted ancestors. You could not stand to be poor in America without the comfort of knowing all those years you resisted the Romans.'

'You're a clod,' said Iorwerth, red in the face. 'A lying, fat, empty-headed clod.' With a glare at laughing Will he collected the drinks and went back to the piano.

'Plenty of ambition with the women has Iorwerth,' said Will. 'Like his father. There is a man—his father. Nearly seventy he was when Iorwerth was born. Fourteen children. Oldest older than me. Has lived here longer than anyone and knows more about people than anyone too. If anyone knows of a man who is lost, it is Ianto . . . MOVE YOUR BLOODY ELBOW OUT OF MY BEER,' he shouted at a man smelling of cattle.

Wedged into the corner the bar made with the fireplace wall, Will and Morgan had to hold their elbows out over the bar in order to get their glasses to their lips. Talk was coming easily and pints were going down more slowly. All the time men coming and going. Near the fire two old ladies with foxtails and dumpling hats sat happily in a pool of composure as they sucked their gums and steadily sipped milk stout. At the piano boys were sneaking arms around the girls who pretended not to notice. Two twos were playing darts, and beer bets were being called. Someone tapped Morgan on the shoulder.

'Is this your pork pie?' the man asked.

'It looks a bit like it,' Morgan said.

The man handed it over and Morgan examined the thumb indentations. Will shook his head but Morgan bit into it. He chewed for a moment then suddenly laughed and could not stop, and pie flakes sprayed across the bar. Will laughed too and put his arm about Morgan's shoulders and called him Butty, then surprised Maggie by buying a round.

'Pooh!' Will suddenly exclaimed and stood straight. 'Who blew a stinky?' He looked accusingly at a group of three tall, sombre men who stood silently together.

'Not me,' grunted one.

'You more like it,' said another.

The third looked away.

'Disgusting!' Will said. Then in a whisper he added, 'Parry's brothers. Live over the hill from you. Mean. To be avoided. Keep to themselves, and think only they are right. Make their own rules. And like now—you cannot trust them.'

Morgan felt full so he went outside for a leak. In the dark he fumbled forward and someone said, 'Watch out for my back pocket.' They did a few steps around each other before the other man went inside. Morgan yawned as he stood there looking up from under the shed at the stars in a sky which seemed to be in movement.

That is the place to be, he whispered, up there in the sky or whatever it is called between stars. Moving leisurely and without deviation on some pre-ordained course, like a sun-ship with sails of gold, watching all those far-out creatures, hearing all that distant music. Wings, colours, cloud fountains; worlds trading fours with each other, echoes and variations bounding from one to the other: vapour changing, forming solids, coming together, disintegrating—

creation, destruction, all observed, not experienced. Immortality! Yet just now there would be no one there.

These people would never be happy on that golden boat . . . was Grando ever at the *Rose and Crown*?

He wiggled it and buttoned up and went inside. Standing next to Will was an ancient man who looked like a bundle of pipe-cleaners. He was introduced as Ianto Davies, Iowerth's father.

'What will you drink, Mr Davies?' Morgan asked.

'Ianto is my name,' he said. 'Ianto. I do not like people to suggest that falling down dead I will be any moment. Bitter if you please.'

Morgan ordered the beer and refills for Will and himself.

'Here's to Wales,' said Morgan.

'Here's to you,' said Ianto Davies.

'Here's to rust and corrosion, shit and corruption,' said Will, weaving.

'There is odd the Americans are, leaving their money on the bar like that,' said Ianto. After drinking, he went on, 'There used to be a Rhydderch family had a farm here. Nice people. They left for London to sell milk in the war with the Kaiser.'

'Not the man. Twenty years ago, when I saw him last, he lived in the Rhondda. He was about sixty then. Maybe older. He moved up this way later.'

'What was he like?' Ianto asked.

'Tall, black hair, teeth like piano keys. Large hands. Wide-open blue eyes.'

'Was he a miner?'

'Yes, but no scars on him.'

'Why would he, a miner, come to Dyfnaint?'

Morgan shrugged. 'Maybe he just got tired of coal-dust.'

85

'Not married was he?'

'No—but he loved children.' Then the rest spilled out. 'They said that he was intense, incorruptible, always reading, always arguing over the meaning of things. He liked to talk, talk. My old man was the local leader with the Federation and Grando Rhydderch was always behind with the sense, working out and deciding what was right, what was honest, what was ethical. He was angry at my old man for leaving at a time the miners needed him most.'

'So your father was a miner also?'

'Yes but with a businessman's mind. Guts they said but not too honest.'

'Good friends often love each other for what they themselves do lack,' said Ianto.

Then Will fell off his stool. He had been drinking with two groups at once, and, trying to find out whose turn it was to buy, he had leaned too far. He was sprawled on the floor and Morgan went to help him up but he too felt dizzy and Ianto had to assist him. 'I've got double-breasted feet,' Will said when they finally got him up. He rubbed his forehead where already a blue egg was appearing. Ianto frowned then ignored him.

'Twenty-five years ago,' Ianto said, head back, staring at the ceiling. 'Let me see. Glyndwr came from Bangor. He died. Then the Evanses and Twm-Shon-the-mole, and then the Merfyn Joneses. Later there were soldiers to the north and the south, and observer men to watch for the aeroplanes, and then came the prisoners of war. The gypsies stayed a bit with Twm Shon. People always going on. The English colonel and his lady. Not staying. And Jones-Motor-Engine —killed himself driving into Cwm Lake.'

'Who's Twm-Shon-the-mole?' Morgan asked.

'He's a traveller like yourself,' Will mumbled. 'At least he was once.'

'He came here from South Wales,' said Ianto, 'but not like your man at all. Blind now, withered. A bit peculiar...'

'Peculiar!' shouted Will. 'He's not peculiar! Not a book-man like Morgan's man but not peculiar by a long chalk.'

'Will is his friend,' said Ianto. 'Twm is more or less a hermit and you know how people act when they have only themselves for company. Blind he is but manages wonderful. Gardens he does, snares rabbits, catches fish, chops wood. And he tells tales.'

Will made a disgusted noise with his lips.

Ianto finished his drink and pulled himself upright. 'A pity it is your man is not now here, Morgan. But have Will Twice take you to see Howell Powell. If your Mr Rhydderch came and passed on, one way or the other, he could find out for you. A good nose has Howell.' He squinted at his son who was a little unsteady, and with a curt goodnight was gone.

Will, waiting for Morgan to finish his drink, just then drank someone else's beer and was caught at it, and there was some pushing about and some nifty elbow and shoulder work before the victim was pacified by the buying of another beer. It was now too crowded for the dart players to throw, and Maggie, flushed and wet under the arms, got so busy that she allowed Will to help her. Morgan bought a round of drinks for Iorwerth and his friends and the young people, serious but pleased, raised their glasses to him and sang him a song where the melody was handled by the piano and the descant by the singers. Everyone listened for this but as soon as it was over the talk started up again.

Morgan, nearing the juice level, had slowed his drinking,

for nothing was where he knew it to be, nor was it as it should be. There was no control of anything, not even of his bladder. After a while it was up again and out again, and now the stars were blurred and he noticed the stink, and his leg got wet, and the back passage was dark and depressing. But what was worse was the loss of dignity just when he valued it most . . .

'Willie,' he called across the bar, 'no one seems to know how important it is to know the importance of everything.'

'Right you are, boyo,' said Willie. 'A light should come on or a gong should sound to stop the bright moment from slipping by.'

Life is just as it is, that is its trouble, thought Morgan. Like that night before they left for America. There was gaiety and festivity and speeches, some funny, some grave: there were trembling lips and noble tears and strong hands—like hell, like hell! It was a day of no school but no one to see for the others were attending, and the quiet the oh so mournful morning quiet, followed by an evening of silent packing, then when Grando came, shrieks from his mother, and his father was quiet and sort of drawn tight around the mouth, and he was sent to bed and he crouched with his ear to the wall. His mother saying sneering things, and Grando saying 'Are you sure it is your choice? Are you sure then?' and not taking yes for an answer . . .

'Time, Gentlemen,' Maggie called. There was a hurried reordering.

Time! He tried a laugh. Time to stop, to change, to start something else. Remember, as a child, the hundred questions on a page and a bell tinkles and you've got to turn the page

88

and you haven't done seventy. And there before you is another hundred questions, and before you've done ten of these you can hear the tinkling just about to go off. And remember Lawrence Henry who made a glider with the question sheet after the first tinkling and when the second tinkling came he stood up on his chair and laughed and launched the glider out over us all and we watched as it swooped and banked and even climbed for MINUTES before coming down into an inkpot. He laughed. Of course out he went on his earhole. And it upset all the bells for the rest of the period. I got eighty-seven questions answered before one of the bells went off. Lawrence Henry! Tut! He hanged himself in a barn . . .

'Time. Time Gentlemen Please.'
Talk lagged and then continued with upperlip-licks in unison. Will pulled himself a free one and gave Maggie a little cuddle. A few empty glasses were deposited on the bar and there were a few calls of goodnight. Then Morgan heard Gwylan's voice.
'Drunk again, Dada?'
'Just been out in the sun too long, love,' he said.
She made a face at Morgan's glumness.
'Hello love,' he said.
'Hello,' she said. She stood close to him with her back against the bar watching the men leave.
Maggie kept it up. 'Time Gentlemen. Time.'
'Do you like your new room?' Gwylan asked.
He grinned. 'It's not so convenient.'
She turned her head away, and he shook his to clear it. 'Going to get kicked out of here,' he said, but she went 'sssh'.
Maggie shepherded the last of the customers out—'Good-

night, goodnight, goodnight'—and locked the door. Gwylan left the bar and poked the fire, then sat near it and Maggie joined her. Outside there were the fading cries of goodnight, and then quiet.

'The dead feeling after a ball,' Morgan said to break the quiet.

'The good feeling,' Maggie said. She smiled as she pushed back her hair, a fine dew on her moustache. 'It was a good evening. Oh, Willie Will I would like a nip.' She sighed and fanned herself and exchanged a soft smile with Gwylan.

Will came weaving with the bottle and four glasses. 'All legs and wings I am,' he said. He poured the black rum and without a word they held up their glasses, nodded, and sipped.

'What now, Morgan?' Will asked.

'I'll think about it another day.'

'Are you enjoying your search, Mr Johns?' asked Maggie.

'Yesterday I wasn't, but today off-and-on I am.'

'I am glad you like us,' she said.

Gwylan took a sip but did not take her eyes from the fire.

'You do not know us yet, boy,' said Will.

'Who knows who—or what,' Morgan said. He went to the upright and tried a chord, then worked over the song they had given him.

'Help me with the glasses, Will,' Maggie said.

'Righto,' said Will.

They seemed content enough.

Standing, Morgan played around hesitantly, then sat down and played the tune as it was, then did it his way. Gwylan stood against his back, and after a while he found he could play it well enough with one hand. Then he stopped and grinned.

'Entertainments tax, you know,' he said.

'I liked that,' she said. 'Is that the way it usually comes out for you?'

He shrugged, but nodded.

'Play again.'

But he got up and picked up a set of darts. 'I should spend more time with stuff like this,' he said. 'Means less.'

He threw the first dart and it stuck in the wall three feet from the board. He made a noise that could have been a laugh if it had had some humour in it. The second dart just nicked the outer wire ring. The third dart hit the board half-way to the bull's-eye. 'That's the story of my life,' he said. 'Aim for fifty and get seventeen.'

'In that section it counts triple,' Gwylan said. 'You aimed for fifty and got fifty-one.'

'How about that.'

'Let us go,' she said.

Seeing them ready to leave, Will came around the bar and put his hands on Morgan's shoulders. 'Take care of her,' he said.

'Will,' said Gwylan, 'you are an old fool.'

'An old fool you are at that,' said Maggie, pleased.

Will laughed and said, 'You will be sorry, Morgan, that you ate that pie.'

*　　*　　*　　*　　*

He could just see the road before him but when they left it near the chapel he was lost, so he did not look, trusting her as they walked, swishing the grasses, across the field. Stars were faint and the moon was covered by cloud, and only sometimes could he see a tree against the sky. Together they squeezed through a turnstile and he held her there but she turned her face and slipped through the gate, holding him in, then running into the darkness. He called to her and followed, but could see nothing.

He called again, softly, his head up. There was a rustle of grass and he rushed towards the sound, and, scrambling around, touched her leg and followed it. He fell forward over her as she sat to her shoulders in the grass.

'Let's voluptuate,' he said.

'It's sleep you need,' she answered.

'Then let's sleep.'

'The man who sleeps a night on this mountain awakes a poet or a madman.'

'I remember that. That's all I need.'

'Perhaps it would do you good,' she said.

'Where are we anyway?'

'Above the world,' she said, getting to her feet and pulling him up.

'What a little world you live in. You stand on a molehill and you're elevated.'

'We can be moved by little things,' she said. 'A mountain is a state of mind.'

'What if you saw real mountains?'

'What if I did. After such a height it is incomprehensible but only in size. When you are moved it is incomprehensible in beauty.'

'You'd be impressed enough,' he said. 'In the valley it's hot enough to change your shape, but up above there's always snow.'

'I am sure that I would like the mountains. But I am moved to the limit by what is familiar.' She was guiding him through a grove of trees that whispered as they passed.

'You're stubborn.'

'Love is stubborn,' she said.

'Yes? Kind of faithful?'

'It is always there if that is what you mean by faithful—even if you are almost eaten up with other feelings of the moment.'

Then, below them, were the village lights, each one coloured by drawn curtains . . . The grass was damp but sweet smelling.

'Any snakes?' he asked.

'Only gentle ones.'

'How come it's so warm?

'The land is going—crazy,' she said.

'Crazy!' he answered. 'Warm and dark. I bet all kinds of shady goings-on are going on.'

'That is nice,' she said, 'if they are enjoyed.'

'The lights are pretty . . . Will isn't home yet.'

'Maggie's sister has a hard time getting rid of him. He will not grow up.'

'My old man wouldn't either—but the result was different,' Morgan said. 'But the country he left was never like this.'

'What was it like to him?'

'He said that all he could remember were the breadlines with the pits closed down and tuberculosis hovering near, and tight rows of houses like tombstones in the rain.'

'That is Wales also. Was he never sorry he left?'

'Never. He was glad to be away. I grew up to the refrain "There was never a land like this"—meaning America.' Morgan felt for cigarettes but had none. With his hands behind his head he stretched out. 'I don't know whether I like success. Like he made money with hardware, joined clubs and barked loudly in them, got fat and smoked cigars, but he never made a decision in his life after deciding to emigrate. Maybe he left something here.'

'Is he dead now?'

'That's why I'm here. A death-bed promise with a roomful of pity. Maybe he thought that Grando could give me wisdom at least in proportion to the money he left me. Sure-gulp-feller, I said. Embarrassed all to hell because he was crying real weak tears. He looked so goddamn miserable.'

'Don't you ever cry, Morgan?'

'No.'

'You poor man. Oh you have forgotten how to cry.'

A small wind nosed through the grasses like a mouse. When she came down to him her hair fell onto his face.

CHAPTER SIX

THE GHOSTS in me and in this house! I call them again, again in the mask of night but with no answer. The house settles itself as the world turns in its sleep, and timbers creak when I am not listening and hold their ancient breath when I stop mine to hear.

Men's voices lost-calling for their childhood and crying for their loss in the night, and snores and rumbles and moans and ohs. The long ohs that had turned them grey in the face and had glazed their eyes. 'You would be surprised what an old woman of eighty-two dreams about,' Grandma had said. But then, for her, there had been nightly compensation for the day. Would I be surprised at what old men dream of? I will ask them and watch their faces. Will a smile of fear flit over and away? Will I be able to listen when they lie?

Lost old men sharing a bed and a chamber pot, who shave each morning with no wish. Who killed you, Rhys? Who pierced your heart, Thomas? Who spat hot in your eyes, Emlyn? Shall I show you what you were? Or is there kindness in a forced reverence? No, for that is a silent applause with a cruel lie abobbing before the eyes of the soul.

Young boys eight years in life laugh in their sleep, and even in their indecisive night walking, pull royal bedclothes in a train of hope behind them. They speak volubly in a language near the spinning centre of life. Their dragons and their princes, their castles and their caves, the swirl of dream seas and the red rocks are in their life which is day and night. Night awakening and day dreaming. They reach plump hands through the scum, down deep into the green to the goldfish darting. Look for the boy, old man . . .

Sleep had been clamouring and now the wide-awake was like a fable.

There was a moon which came in sweeps and went in flashes as if on wings, and in the dark the light made he saw the clouds tumbling in colours as if over the burning boy. He saw figures—not formulated with arms and legs or wings and tails—but merely figures dancing on the hills with sea-mist horses.

And a dog with a white throat walked in silence across the farm's face and up towards the dance. 'Wait for the moon to fall and for the sun to rise,' he heard. Change was slow. Morgan dressed and quietly left the house and climbed the hill and watched the night go home.

And the night was not alone.

As he stood against a tree within the valley's rim he saw a man come up from the woods at the river's turning. In black with long legs and arms that jerked, and with his head bent low and with a wide hat upon it. He walked close and quickly by, but gave no greeting. Then Morgan saw two sister figures coming from the woods where the river turned. They came—two, thin, huddling, narrow-skirted women shawled and scarved, not looking at each other, not looking at the sky, not looking at the earth, not looking. Part of the way of the man in black they walked then turned over the lip of the valley towards another bay. South-walking.

At intervals of half the valley's length (from river-turning woods to curve away of hills) there came six people. Some came with steps that danced on the earth with eyes on the sky, and some came hiding from themselves. None lingered long. When all, he thought, had gone, a girl came in the early morning. A girl almost a woman. She lingered near where the trees ended, then, running, she came towards the house. The sun was now before him and she saw him in the light against the tree. Her steps faltered, became sedate, and she watched him as she came nearer.

Then she nodded and he said hello and she replied the same. He remarked about the beauty of the day and she said yes and smiled and passed him and went back to the house he had left.

She was the last of seven who came from the woods at the turning of the river before the sun turned up.

*   *   *   *   *

Morgan went into breakfast and sat on the smooth bench across from the three farmhands.

Rhys with calm face and his hands held before him like a child said, 'For what we are about to receive may the Lord make us truly thankful.'

Thomas, with spit on his chin, followed with a cough and a mumbling and a 'make the true Lord thankful'.

Emlyn, his eyes screwed up like walnut shells and his hands clenched between his knees, whispered a long 'A-a-a-amen.'

97

Parry squeezed a blackhead from his nose and said, 'These old men cannot work, cannot sleep quietly, cannot talk sense, cannot die yet. All they can do is eat. Eat, eat, eat, eat, eat. No wonder they pray for it.'

'Tut, tut, Llew,' said Mrs Parry, pouring tea. 'There is a thing to say. Have some bacon, Emlyn.'

'No.'

'Well take milk in your tea then, and pass it up,' said Parry.

'No.'

'Stupid—give it me.'

Emlyn's lips going no no no as Parry reached in front of him. An old man saying no no no too late in life. Slowly, giving Morgan plenty of time to avoid his look if he wished, Emlyn moved his eyes across at him. A whining came out of his throat and his eyes were bright and Morgan felt a sadness as when he saw a bird a-flutter with a dangling wing, and he was ashamed of the pity he felt. When Emlyn's eyes reached Morgan, he spoke in a soft voice that went up and down, ending up.

'I saw a man fall under the moon and there was blood everywhere,' Emlyn said.

'Jesus,' said Parry. He stood over the man, shaking his head and absently probing his tongue around at the back of his clacking teeth.

Morgan let his face relax and nodded at the man across the table. The sick, bright shine left Emlyn's eyes and he began to eat, using his hands and a pocket knife. Morgan, though now with little hunger, took a boiled egg from a bowl and cracked it and scooped it from its shell onto his toast.

The boy and the girl, laughing at secrets, came into the

kitchen but offered no chance for hellos. They did not speak and Morgan felt in the way, and it was worse when Emlyn said, 'Birds do not sing here anymore do they, Thomas.' Thomas said nothing; he just sat and chewed and looked at Parry with red-rimmed eyes.

Parry said, 'What passes for conversation with you, Emlyn, passes all understanding.' He was alone when he laughed.

The yellow oilcloth that covered the table was worn in creases and the grey cloth backing showed through. Rhys, with the heel of one hand rubbing at his eye, followed the pattern of creases with the thumb of his other hand and everyone watched as he went round and round as if in a maze, always returning to the same central hole. Then the boy lifted his spoon high, brought it down with a crack on his brown egg, and sang out 'BONG'—and Morgan was in and the father was out.

'I would like to lay an egg,' Owen said.

'Don't talk like a fool,' said his father.

'What colour egg?' asked his sister.

'Don't encourage the boy with his baby talk,' said the father.

'A purple egg—all shiny.'

'Would you eat it?'

'No.'

'Would it ever hatch out?'

'Of course. I would sit on it for three days and a couple of nights and it would pink pink pink and hatch out.'

'What would it be?' Morgan asked.

The father blurted out, 'Don't encourage the boy if you please. I want him to grow up like his father and be a man, and here he is talking like a little girl.'

'Anyway,' said the boy, 'it would be wonderful. It would start off ugly and grow lovely.'

'Like a frog into a knight?' Morgan asked. Parry snorted.

'No, not a frog, and not a knight. A cross-eyed lizard that turns into a dragon more lovely than a hundred horses and all covered in golden armour and I would tame it and it would do things and be useful.'

'Christ!' exploded the father. 'Give me some more tea.'

'Shush, Llew,' said the mother.

In a whisper, with his lips against his milk glass, the boy said, 'Mr Christ, please give me some more tea.' And, just to be taking sides, Morgan laughed, and the boy was surprised into laughing with him.

'All this house will end up in a Ninstitution,' said the father.

'Mrs Evans-the-coal is having two new babies,' Owen said.

'Don't gossip,' said the father.

'It is not gossip,' said the boy. 'She knows all about it. It can't be gossip if she *knows* about it. She carries them inside her to stop the hobgoblins putting berry juice on their eyes.' He laughed. 'And when she sits down they sit down and when she bends over they . . .'

'Oh stop it. You are like an old woman,' said his father.

'Why like an old woman?'

'And there are no such things.'

'There are no such things what?' asked Owen.

'Hobgoblins you call them.'

'What! No hobgoblins?'

'No.'

'Where is there no hobgoblins?' Laughter dribbled at the corners of the boy's mouth.

'Nowhere, nowhere.'

'Nowhere there is no hobgoblins? No hobgoblins in Dyfnaint?'

'No, no, no gobhoblins . . . no boghoblins nowhere.'

'Who said so?'

'I said so.'

'I seen them,' said the boy, and his eyes shone and there was laughter full on his lips. 'I know where they live. I seen them go there. Red they are and Enid-the-shop said that there is women hobgoblins too but she is such a liar you cannot tell.'

'Stop it, stop it,' said Parry. 'Lies, lies, lies all day long. You are getting to be a fool, boy. You will end up like Emlyn here.'

'Emlyn,' said the boy, 'please pass me the milk.' When he did so the boy ran two stiff fingers like legs up the old man's hand.

Emlyn said, 'Once a big white bird came to the river but after one day it flew away.'

'It was a swan,' said Owen.

'It was a heron,' said Mair.

'It was a white donkey with flying ears,' said Owen.

'It was a ghost,' said Morgan.

'I saw a ghost last night,' Owen said into his glass, his voice muffled. 'Clump, clump, clump, it came down the stairs. Snicker, snicker, snicker across the floor. Creak, creak, creak out through the door, and I peeped through the bedroom window and I saw it cross the yard and go up the hill.'

The girl's eyes were on Morgan and there was fear there and her hands were together.

'That was me, Owen,' Morgan said. 'Early this morning I went out for a walk.'

'I know it was you,' the boy said, 'but I saw the ghost that followed you over the hill.' He stood up, ran to his sister and then out into the sun and the dogs came to him.

Parry shouted after him, 'Don't forget what I told you. You keep away from that William-Williams-the-fish. Do you hear?' But the boy was gone.

His sister, without smiling, said, 'He frightened himself.' And Morgan answered, 'I'd be afraid too if I saw a man and then a ghost, for then I'd wonder whether there was a man there after all.'

'Such rubbish you are all talking,' said Parry. He lifted the lid of the stove and spat at the fire but missed and it sizzled on the stove top. 'That boy is getting too hupperty. I've been lax. The trouble with children is that they are like wild animals—not trained. They do not know what they should do but they don't like the sound of someone telling them what is right.'

'Some animals never can be trained, I hear,' said Morgan.

'Do not believe it. A springy stick from the hedge and a firm voice—oh they recognize well enough the man who knows how things should be. They try to run sometimes but you just keep at them snicking them around the legs. You have to teach them their lesson, teach them their place, that is the secret. And when they finally do what you want them to do, you show them that you are not as bad as they think. You give them a little tidbit. They like that—but mind you, you mustn't overdo it. Kindness is a curse sometimes. Often I have to watch myself to make sure I do not spoil them. Killing by kindness is a fact, believe me. Kindness can get you in a tight spot sometimes.'

The hired men got up and left the room.

'You have to plan ahead,' Parry went on. 'Think all the

time. Don't let your heart govern. I've got a soft heart really but I hide it. Wouldn't do any good. I'm a regular softy. But people take advantage of you as soon as they see that, so I hide it. Like those men. Really stupid they are—you know how I got them?'

Morgan spread marmalade on a piece of toast and bit into it, then forked up a piece of egg.

'Egg and marmalade together!' Parry cried out. 'You people!' He laughed and shook his head. 'But do you know how I got them? Dumb Emlyn and Company?'

'With a net?'

'They came from a lunatic asylum. A dingy house. All three of them. There it was I took pity because they cried all the time and I felt sorry for them so I took them away.'

'Then they lived happy ever after,' Morgan said.

'They did. We didn't.'

Morgan pushed away his plate. 'Tragedy,' he said.

Parry nodded. 'Here they do no work, and they eat like starving pigs and all we get from them is their old age pension.'

'I hear someone chopping wood steadily enough for one who doesn't get paid for it.'

'What you mean? Well now wait a minute . . .'

'Now Llew,' said Mrs Parry with a nervous haha in her voice. Her daughter stood, still, near the door.

'Y'know they are not human, these men,' Parry said. 'They are stupid like animals. Ignorant. You heard Emlyn with no sense at all all through the meal.'

Morgan put a cigarette in his mouth, letting it dangle while he looked at Parry. He struck the match, inclined his head to light the cigarette, then inhaled deeply and blew smoke in Parry's direction. He got up without answering.

'Is your tea nice then, Mr Johns?' Mrs Parry asked.

'Yeah,' he grunted, finishing it. The girl at the door frowned.

'Oh that is nice,' said Mrs Parry. 'It is nice to have everything nice.'

*   *   *   *   *

Morgan said to Emlyn, 'Come with me to the top of the rise.' Emlyn looked around as if afraid, then came. On the hill they stood looking down into the woods. The sun was in a mackerel sky and the wind was in the trees.

'What is down in the woods, Emlyn?' Morgan asked.

'Bridges.'

'Do they have names?'

'The Bridge of Evil . . . no . . . of Sin . . . and other bridges.'

'Who lives there?'

'Mr Parry says the devil.'

'Are there houses?'

'No.'

'Do you go down there often?'

'No, no, never . . . sometimes.'

'I can hear water fall,' Morgan said.

'I can hear it,' said Emlyn.

They stood with the smelling sea-wind blowing, Emlyn with tears on his face and laughter in his throat.

*   *   *   *   *

'Do you have a treasure?' the boy asked.

Morgan said, 'No,' but he had to think before replying.

'I do,' Owen said.

'At least I don't have any with me.'

'Mine is buried but I dig it up almost every day to look at it.'

'I always forget where I keep mine,' Morgan said.

'I will never be like that.'

'I don't think you will.'

'My treasure is on an island. It is called Cormorant Rock. It is not really an island but when I was small I thought it was an island. You can walk out to it when the tide is out.'

'Maybe you'd show it to me before I leave.'

'All right. I've got a piece of slate—an old arrow head I think it is—and a blue glass stone with a hole in it, the kind a king would wear around his neck on a string, and a red shell with markings like writings washed up from the sea, and a bird's egg in a jewel box, and a foreign coin. And my two front teeth. I've only just started collecting.'

'I don't remember what I've got,' Morgan said.

The boy sat on his heels and the dogs came up and he put his arms around them. 'Tomorrow we are going fishing again, Willie and me,' he said. 'All day we'll be gone. Can you come?'

'I'd like to.'

'Mackerel we usually get, and sometimes flatfish.'

'Fine.'

★　★　★　★　★

The stepping-stoned snake coiled round and round the hill and Morgan took slow steps from one vertebra to another. Around and around the hill, going higher and higher, now

105

towards the sea, now towards the mountains, now towards the village in a haze of seabreak. At the nipple of the hill were two stone eyes and Morgan stood on them, legs astride with the lovely morning about him.

Near the stone eyes and stone tongue was a boulder balanced on a small part of itself. At one time perhaps it moved with the wind or was rocked as men chanted, but now stones and earth were stuck beneath it. Sheltered by it from the wind was a flat stone with a groove down one side and the flat stone shone smooth but for sharp incisions across it.

Morgan faced the woods, and the noise of the falling water was loud and a mist hung over the trees and he saw three bridges, one above the other, straddling the river before it fell. The bottom bridge was straight and of rotting logs, the second bridge an arc of finished wood but white with mould, and the third was a simple bridge of stone. Across the bridge went a narrow country road that connected Dyfnaint with another coastal town to the south. But, following the nod of the snake's head, Morgan went down into the wood. Into the dimness where the trees dripped and grey lichen grew.

The path dithered like an indecisive stream but the thunder of the water became steady and only a nearby dripdrip marred the comfort of the one noise. There were no birds, and no dusty sun streamed through the branches. The down fall of the path stopped at a clearing where the trees were dead and wet and black and standing straight. Across the clearing the mist rolled, and Morgan walked through it and saw the water falling. Where the water slowly rolled under the bridges and over the falls, the sun shone and the water was white and the mist had many colours.

But did seven people come for the moon in the water?

Morgan followed the river and the path dipped down as the river raced on towards the sea. Around a black-rocked bend the dropping of the river stopped and the water swirled round and round in a smooth punchbowl, and the water was black and deep with floating spume. And the water was as if in two cupped hands and it ran out between the thumbs. The colour of the day was blue and not grey, though there was in the blue, green and yellow and black and white, and even red. And the sun, though weak, was not without warmth. He knelt and took water in his hands and sipped. Bubbles came up from the dark pool as if from some slow exhalation.

Below the punchbowl Morgan sat on a rock, flat like a brown pitted nipple, and took out his flute. After listening to the sound of water he blew a double note, repeated it and was off, and the water was like a left hand or a steady bass. As he played he dropped his head. Once he stopped as if waiting for someone but then went on and sang a bit.

But suddenly he stopped and looked across the river. An old, thin man stood on a ledge above the river pointing at Morgan with a crooked stick. The old man's face was pale with knobs of bone under sunken eyes. He wore a rough coat buttoned to the throat and he carried a cage made of twigs. In the cage was a red ferret with a white breast.

Morgan shouted a hello.

The man tilted his head but that was all, and only then did Morgan realize how loud was the roar from the falls. The old man waited and then held up the cage to his neck, and his lips moved. Then, the cage still held high and the stick held before him, he turned and walked on—along the narrow ledge above the water and around the bend of the cliff.

Round and round went the dark water in the black hands.

Morgan put the flute back in his pocket and returned the way he had come.

★   ★   ★   ★   ★

'I went down into the woods where you walked this morning,' Morgan said to Mair.

'Indeed.'

'Does anyone live down there?'

'Not in the woods.'

'I saw a man near the falls who looked as if he knew his way around. He had a ferret in a cage and he was talking to it.'

'That was nice for it,' she said, looking over her shoulder at the house.

'You're not being very helpful.'

'I would if I could but you know that I can't,' she said. 'I do not know why you ask—I mean, what you want. I do not know why you are here.' She smoothed her hair and threw back her head, then tried for composure, and was more or less successful at it.

'What if I said I was writing a book?'

'Well then lies would do just as well,' she said, an adult manner putting more than an edge to her voice. 'But we want to tell the truth, if truth we know. Though if we do not know there is no purpose in talking about it.'

Morgan smiled. For the first time she avoided his eyes.

'I will have to leave you now,' she said. 'I have to go to the village.'

'I'll walk with you. I'd like to know more. It's not often I annoy someone by saying so little.'

'I will ask my father if you may walk with me,' she said.

'Do that.'

She turned quickly and went into the house but was gone but a moment. When she returned she carried a basket which she held before her as if for protection. Her well-washed dress was too small for her so that it showed her knees and pulled tight under her arms and across her young breasts, straining the buttons. Her shoulders were bare, and as she walked to the gate she tossed her head so that her hair moved over her shoulders like seafronds over a rock. Morgan caught up with her and took her stride. The top of her head was below the level of his chin.

'Now where were we?' he said. 'It seemed that I said not much of anything and then you shot fire and ice down your nose at me. Shouldn't a visitor's interest give you pleasure?'

'I hope indeed you are enjoying your visit,' she said.

'I am, sort of, although some do not seem to be happy that I'm here. Someone who does seem quite happy about it said that I ask too many questions. Do you think that could be it?'

'Perhaps.'

'Do you think that they are afraid to answer questions?'

'Why should we be afraid?' She rested her free hand on her hip and hunched her shoulder towards her chin. It was a woman's gesture though the hand was that of a child—pale and without character, dirty with ragged fingernails.

'Why? There could be all kinds of reasons. Fear of reprimand, fear of ridicule, fear of getting hurt, fear of losing something . . .'

'There is nothing to be afraid of here,' she said, a flash of fear in her eyes.

'I guess fear is too strong a word,' he said, smiling, yet ashamed of the understanding-adult role that was so easily available. 'But like now—what arouses my curiosity at this moment has nothing to do with the why I'm here. But I'm here so I might as well make the most of it.'

'I do not know what it is you want.'

'I don't want much. Nothing as large as truth, don't fear.'

'As I say,' she said, 'there is nothing to fear.'

'Then can I ask the questions?'

'I will do my best.'

'Do you often go walking in the mornings?'

'I go sometimes,' she said. Her hand went up to her face, a finger exploring the corner of her mouth. (Then he remembered, 'But, Grando, what is it that hurts?' 'It is your innocence, child. You'll learn to hate it for the trouble it brings.')

'Where do you go?' he asked. ('They want you because of that innocence, child. They keep after you. And even those who admire it, hope, all the time, that you do not have it.')

'Here and there,' she replied.

'I saw so many people out early this morning,' Morgan said.

'In the country that is quite natural.'

He dropped the hook. 'Someone told me that the people of Dyfnaint worship the night.'

And she took it. 'Oh that is wicked.' She stopped and stamped her foot twice. 'There is nothing sinful here.'

'Oh I believe it, yet . . .'

'It is America that is sinful, Americans who are wicked.

My father says that they are foolish and boastful like little boys.'

'That's as true as saying that all Wales is dark and primitive and superstitious,' Morgan said.

'You have no way of knowing what Wales is to me. Why should I put words to it? It is my life.'

Morgan chuckled, for annoyance's sake. 'Maybe you could take me for a walk one early morning. If it is a good experience then it will be something of value to take home.'

'I must leave you here,' she said, and turned off the path and walked away with long-legged stride across the field. Her hair was blowing in the wind and her cheeks were pink. She walked with her head up as if she knew where she was going, but only a dozen steps away from the path she stumbled and fell forward onto one hand. She was up immediately and running, now sure-footed.

CHAPTER SEVEN

'A BIG sign there is—Howell-Powell-Can't-Miss-It.' But where? Morgan walked up one side of the street, down the other. People watched though now some nodded at him briefly before looking away. Up the street again, this time looking across at the buildings . . . It was like in old stories where the signposts were always half hidden by weeds or vines, sometimes only carved on trees or scratched on rocks, sometimes even with no written word but a talking jackdaw or a frog that speaks in riddles. The smaller the signposts the greater the mission, it used to be.

But there it was—Howell Powell LL.B.—in peeling gold letters across the bottom half, painted black, of an upstairs window. The way up was a narrow stairway between the grocer's and the ironmonger's, and Morgan took it. At the top of the stairs was a frosted glass door and a green brass plate with the name on it.

He knocked, and to a 'come in', went in. Near the window, a nimble, red-hairy man seemed to be hiding behind large glasses and a big black pipe. On the window-pane was a mist of breath and the imprint of a nose.

'Mr Johns? Howell Powell,' said Howell Powell, making things clear. He pushed a straight, stubby finger against the bridge of his glasses, before taking Morgan's hand and wagging it about.

'Mr Davies suggested that I see you.'

'Yes, indeed. He told me about your intentions. A much more interesting case for me than defending someone who waters their milk or rides a bicycle without a rear light. Comes no oftener than once in a life.' He hunched back up his big tweed coat which had slipped on his thin shoulders in the hand-shaking.

'Do you think you can help?'

'Certainly. The best man I am for the job. Partly because of my position which is convenient, and partly because of my disposition which is foul. Sit down, please.'

The leather chair squeaked and swooshed out dust as it received him.

'Can I offer you a little whisky? If it is not too early in the day.'

'Thanks,' said Morgan. 'It's seldom too early.'

A bottle was produced from a green and dented filing cabinet, glasses from the yellow-varnished roll-top. Howell Powell elbowed away a sausage-box of till rolls and a confusion of papers, and poured. He passed the drink, ducking with the grace of habit around a strip of fly-paper which hung, stiff with the flies of last summer, from the lampshade.

The gas fire, set in a marble fireplace with Corinthian columns, did a cool chorus of pops and whistles. Above it a group of moustached and high-collared deacons looked grimly down, one seeming to point with a surreptitious thumb to the certificate in an adjacent frame. On the mantelpiece between a small ship in a bottle and a large one in a case, was a porcelain clock with a brass ticker that jigged with some irregularity.

Behind the desk was a calendar with the picture of a bull and a pig with the pronouncement JONES THE BUTCHER ALL THE BEST MEATS.

'Welsh cheesecake,' said the solicitor.

'It's a change,' Morgan said.

'I am sure it is but whether it is welcome I wonder.' Howell Powell took his drink in one swallow and smacked his lips with enthusiasm but he corked the bottle and put it away.

'I don't know whether you'll want the job,' said Morgan, 'when you find out how little there is to go on.'

'Don't worry about it.' He nipped around the desk and bent to the window-pane. 'I am the nosiest man in the county,' he said. 'In my position I enquire into everything, and from my spy-out I can see everything. That is what they dislike most.' His pipe tapped against the glass as he peered down into the street, moving his head about for a better look through the streaks of seagull shit. 'A small town does not offer much, but what it has I know about. I understand you were born in Wales.'

'Yes.'

'Then you know how it is. My father was solicitor here before me. Same office, same furniture, same books. The calendar is new. Solicitor, Auctioneer, *Western Mail* representative and *Cambrian News* reporter. Tax problems dealt with, government yield reports filled out. I know more about Dyfnaint than anyone—but what a boast that is. Yet until you came I was happy enough, and the moment you leave I'll be happy again.' He allowed his pipe to droop, then he straightened himself and his pipe and laughed through it, sending up clouds of ashes. 'I'll find him.'

'It's possible that he's dead.'

'Yes, that too is a way out,' said Howell Powell. 'Oh for the glory that is gone. A natural thing, I think it is, for people to disappear. It is a wonder more do not do it. Even those who cannot disappear would like to live, I do believe, with a cupboard full of plastic faces so that each day it would be get up and choose a face to go out and meet your enemies. I too would like to do that. Oh for the glory that is gone. There is an old tale of two Welsh kings sitting on a rock, boasting one to the other. One said, "See the vast fields I own?" "Where?" asked the other. "Above," said the first, pointing to the night sky. "And do you see all my sheep?" said the second. "Where?" asked the first. "There," said the second, jabbing a finger at the stars. There was silence for a moment then the first king jumped up. "How is it," he shouted, "that your sheep are grazing on my pasture?" So there was a war. Welshmen are not like that any more.'

'You ought to be glad,' Morgan said.

'I am sorry for it. When we have a visitor, I think perhaps in his country men are still like this.'

'I'm afraid they are,' said Morgan.

'That is fine. For greatness often comes that way—with a fine aggression. When it comes it is something in the air, in the blood. It is like a virus. I am sure of it. A wonderful contagious disease. We should all go journeying to get in contact with it. But then—some leaves hang on the vine long after the vine is dead—and that is me.'

'Greatness is a big word you've got hold of,' Morgan said. 'Maybe we should be content with less.'

'But you must agree that there is a certain climate for greatness. Here we do not enjoy this climate now. No wonder the man you search for does want to hide his face.'

'I didn't say he hid: I said I can't find him. And if he heard you talking he'd probably get good and mad and make a speech and say sure greatness breeds greatness, even that there's a climate for it, but he believed . . .' (Did he? Sure he did.) '. . . that anyone could rise out of the lowest place.'

'We need our heroes,' said Howell Powell. 'But where can we find them now, tell me that, Mr Johns. Wales is like a sleeping cat showing only a rolling eyeball and a twitching tail, getting older all the time, dreaming away her middle age—never aware of the scampering mice. And yet her prime is not long gone. Everything had excitement in it just a while ago. In everything we did there was drama. Even in religion, not so long ago, there was drama. One great preacher would arrange all the candles so that one wall of the chapel was in light and when he would shout—and oh he had a voice like trumpets not like tin whistles now—and when he would shout "The Finger of the Lord" he would fling out his hand and the shadow of his arm and the pointed finger would be thrown dark along the wall. Oh there were sighs and whimperings and moans I tell you. They loved it. Life had drama, I say. They believed everything was possible. They wanted surprise—you might say that they were prepared for surprises. But the end was near. Ah yes, your Mr Rhydderch may have come here, but it was in time he should have travelled, not in space.

'I am going to write a book one day. Put the town on the map. History, customs, superstitions, life as it is lived. Of course I couldn't live here any more . . .' The return of good humour reddened his face. 'I will tell you something, Mr Johns—will you stay a while and talk? I always have a cup of tea about eleven—you could join me. Righto. I will tell you something. People think that Wales is only the coal-mines. "How green was my valley." That is what it is like to the world. How green indeed! That is all right but what was it like, look you, before they started to dig up coal and before the English and the others came to the valleys? What was it like? Dyfnaint had a place then, was like a thousand other thriving towns that did not have a Norman castle or a coalmine. Let me tell you the story. One moment.'

He went to the washbasin and juggled the kettle under the tap, partly filling it. Then while he talked, he lit a gas ring near the gas fire and set the kettle on it. From the filing-and-whisky-cabinet he took out cups and a tea caddy.

'If you and your Mr Rhydderch and I were all back a hundred years or so you would really have to use my services. Of course then perhaps there would be no reason for his hiding—yes I know what you said but I know dif-ferent. I know better. A hundred years or so ago I would have to look at the passenger lists on the ships going to America and South Africa and France, and at the coach lists, and at the lists of employees at the lead and silver mines.

'Yes we had our precious metals but do not expect them to be worth your time now. There is no treasure here any more.' He took a paper spill from the pewter pot and got a fresh light from the fire. His cheeks sucked in as he puffed impatiently. 'Perhaps before you go back I could show you the workings—not underground you understand for that would be too dangerous, but where the ore was washed and weighed. There may have been a hundred men and now all is quiet. Dead now, frightening in a way, with just the sound of scampering rats and an occasional falling slate. There is not a hundred men, all told, now working in this entire valley.'

He got up, listened at the door and pulled a dusty blind down and locked the door. 'I thought I heard a client,' he said. He gave a quick laugh, wiped the corners of his mouth, then, eager, went back to his story.

'Small is Dyfnaint. Insignificant. Yet why is it so? Can you imagine it with ships coming and going?'

'No.'

'But true it is. Look!' He dusted the glass case in which was the model of a ship. 'This is one of the two ships that sailed from this very harbour to the New World. It was called *Gwalia*—that means Wales. Twice a year to New York they went. Now look at this.' He went back to the desk and opened a ledger. It had been used as a scrap book and was now opened to a poster dated 1868. The poster gave the captain's name as Hugh Powell.

'My great-grandfather. Hugh Powell. He was the last in my family of a long line of sea captains. Across the oceans regularly he sailed his ship, carrying families and their belongings to the new land. On his last journey he decided to sail around the Horn to San Francisco. He did, and at home I have a print of old San Francisco showing the *Gwalia* in the harbour. He set sail for home but two days out he hit a storm which sank the ship, and all aboard were lost.' He took another book down from the shelf. It was a heavy, leather-bound book with a brass clasp. He held it in the crook of his arm against his chest, but made no motion to show it. 'This is an early log of his. A master of the understated drama he was—the loss of a mast, for instance, took up one line. Only once in this book does he permit a personal note to slip in. "I believe," he wrote, "that all men and women who undertake this voyage are people of courage and are filled with joy." There is beauty for you . . . "and are filled with joy" . . . On those journeys there was no dancing under the stars, no swimming pools, no picture shows or fancy bars.'

The clock clanked eleven times. The tea was poured.

'The sea sometimes is an empty place,' Morgan said, not intending to.

'Courage they needed and courage they had. The people who made that voyage did not make the decision over breakfast. It was a decision they had to live with a bit. Oh they believed in it. They had their heroes. But why they left then I do not know for there was much to be proud of without moving . . . The mines and the smelting works busy, the boatbuilders who built my great-grandfather's vessels with plenty of work, another pub called *The Happy Druid* doing roaring-drunk business, people prospering and a regular coach coming up the coast and on into Aber. It was by no means a metropolis, don't misunderstand, but it was busy enough. A town to be proud of. Now what! San Francisco is a city of the world and around it are a hundred thriving towns . . .'

'Don't knock it too hard . . .'

'I know. The New World! Sad it is to me that with a birth there is often a death.' But he laughed, took a gulp of tea, and lit his pipe again. 'That is my weakness. Only interested am I in places at their peak. I am not interested in great antiquities. The Romans I do not quite believe in. I almost do not believe in the Normans and the Elizabethans. But with a little effort I can see myself living a hundred years back, and enjoying every minute of it. I am no pioneer;

I do not want to build an empire. But at the same time I would like to enjoy the fruits of greatness. I am going to write that book one day.'

'You do that,' said Morgan. 'But I wouldn't want to read it. It's the rise I get my kick from, not the fall.'

The solicitor put the leather-covered book on the table and slid it across. 'A proud man was my great-grandfather, brave and respected. He seemed to find life rewarding. To him life was orderly. Look at his handwriting.'

Morgan took the book: it was heavy and had a water stain on the corner. The pages were yellowed and the ink was a faded brown, but the writing was clear, the words moving across the page evenly and neatly with no words altered or crossed out.

'This is the writing of a man who knew his own mind and was sure of his capabilities,' Howell Powell said.

Morgan nodded.

'I may be wrong,' he went on, 'but it seems that there are few men like that today.'

'Maybe in his time there were few men like him,' Morgan said.

'Perhaps your Mr Rhydderch was such a man?'

'No,' Morgan said. He finished his tea and went to the window. A boat had left the harbour and was dipping over the waves which came from the south-west. The hills across the bay rose up like islands. The village was quiet, the street empty but for a girl hopping on one leg and another one crouched and watching.

Howell Powell joined him at the window. He shook his head at the sight of the empty street, and said, 'Now there is only peace. The end came when we brought back the druids in their silly white sheets, and the silliest head druid would shout, "Is there peace?" and back would come thundering, "There is peace." Can you imagine an America with peace deep down? With inward peace there is no striving—only apathy.'

'You're twisting my arm,' said Morgan. 'Maybe you're also twisting the facts. Dimly remembering it, I used to think it more stirring than a cry of war.'

'Ho I see you are forced into defending us. No need to do that I assure you. I am not that touchy. It is true that we are a sensitive people—I heard somewhere that all defeated nations are sensitive. The Americans, I am told, if you'll pardon it, are not sensitive. Oh if we are anything we are sensitive, but some of us can see well enough to call sour milk sour.' His pipe gurgled so he tapped it out. 'Fancy coming all this way to a place like this. What is it like then, this other place?'

'The things you want to hear about America,' said Morgan, 'are probably true, but you can imagine them better than I can say.' And before the other could press him, he said, 'So you think you can find out what happened to Rhydderch.'

'There are certain avenues to investigate.' Howell Powell, businesslike, dumped the cups into the washbasin and hid the sugar and the tea caddy back in the filing cabinet. 'I would prefer, of course, to have more information to start with. More than the bare facts that he came here, unmarried, twenty or twenty-five years ago at the age of sixty or so.'

'There is no more I can tell you.'

'You cannot place his travels at a more accurate date?'

'No.'

'Do you know his first name?'

'Er—David.'

'No known relatives or friends?'

'No.'

'No reason for changing his name?'

'None that I can imagine.'

'People here have long memories and if it was of no great importance I would take their word and conclude that he never came here. On the other hand, twenty-five years is a long time and in many ways the past twenty-five years have been momentous—even for people in this town. What would you say to five pounds and expenses?'

'You're hired.'

'I'm glad. Few people care any more about anyone's disappearance.'

'Here's ten pounds to go on with.'

'Thank you.' Morgan got up. 'You're not going! Oh well! I can help you well enough but great will be the temptation to prolong the search. Rare it is to meet a man from the outside.'

'Find him or lose him I won't be staying long.'

'I suppose not.' He followed Morgan to the door. 'You know, Mr Johns, we have a tortoise—my son does—or rather he says he does though it stays buried most of the time and we seldom see it—but he says, my son does, that there is no reason for giving it up for dead just because you don't see it around.'

'He sounds a good kid.'

'I suppose so. Come and check up on me in a few days.'

CHAPTER EIGHT

THE REST of the day Morgan spent looking along the banks of the streams and under bridges and across at the mountains of Cader Idris and Plynlimmon, trying to remember . . .

. . . There was a dark gypsy in a green waistcoat with brass buttons and his witch of a wife who did not smell like a mother at all but beautiful in their house on painted wheels. Their baby playing in the dirt with black around his mouth and sparkles in his eyes and no one saying don't. The gypsy came from Spain and knew a duke; his mother was a dancer. He told me so. There was Sunday milk when I stopped and sometimes hazel nuts still green and smelling of hedge leaves, and sometimes honey in the comb. Once a rainbow fish on a stick with the smoke blowing in my eyes. The dark gypsy stole things and kissed his woman on the neck and made her laugh in front of me. Then, back home to sad Sunday dinner and cabbage meat potatoes with a mother's lips thin and a father's face sullen, and knives and forks making clatter. And tears on a sorry Sunday afternoon . . .

. . . Johnny Onions from France (speaking Welsh from Barry Dock) with a crooked cap and Spanish onions on a stick upon his shoulder. 'Catch this,' he said, cocking up his leg and farting fit to kill . . . A woman against the school-house wall with head back and skirts up and legs silver in the moonlight and ohohohohoh to crouching Johnny . . .

. . . 'Before you die you see yourself coming towards you. Always at night and the next day you die.'

Each night I saw me at every corner and across every street: heard my breathing behind my back and felt my fingers against my neck . . .

. . . 'Why doesn't Uncle Dafydd come and visit, Grandma?'

'Bad company he is, boy.'

'Why Grandma?'

'Drinks he does.'

'But Grandpa drinks, Grandma.'

'Hush boy. Uncle Dafydd is a wicked man. With Aunt Blodwen alive drunk up all her money he did and when no more she would give him for smoking, smoke her tea he would. At two shillings a packet. Laugh? No laughing matter, boy. And when for a while him working and your Aunt Blodwen wanting new paper on the walls he says no. Aunty Blodwen does not think he means it so she moves out the furniture into the yard and strips the paper. Bad Uncle Dafydd comes home, throws a tantrum and moves all the furniture back into the stripped house. Four years, until her death, did they live with no paper proper on the walls.'

'I would like to see him everyday, Grandma.'

'Hush boy.'

... Going, and pipes singing and smelling of hot iron, and gas lamps lit all the way down the stone sides and shining on the brass eagle with the book and the coloured glass black and shallow with rain outside, and skinny choirmaster Edwards trembling his yellow beard and chattering his yellow teeth when the organ died. 'Wind, wind, I want wind,' he'd sing as if in anthem, 'Pump, boysbach, pump.' But his pleasure and bad breath and hugging was worse ... And not going and chasing girls with the older boys and sometimes kissing but not liking it much. Running in the churchyard with dull talking going on inside ...

... A pretty afternoon with a bell rocking in a crow-cawed tree tall as a steeple. In the churchyard eating stolen apples green. Stones greymossed and windsmoothed with silly verses and I throwing apple cores at a double bed grave. Then down an avenue of higgledy-piggledy beautiful stones came a preacher like thunder and I ran and ran and hid for a week ...

... Playing hide-and-seek on the boulders under Aber jetty with the slick water coming and going like fear. Finding a good place and no one coming and silence drops with a plip-plopping of water in a green world and cool. 'I am here.' Frightened feet slide over slime and I am shouting, 'You didn't find me,' but wishing all the time that they had ...

... 'Grandma, what are pros-tit-utes?'
'Oops—poop—hoop—WHAT!'
'Pros-tit . . .'
'Never you mind, mind, mind. Give-it-to-me-whatever-it-is-you're-reading-indeed.'

'But I want to read.'

'Read this instead then.'

'Cable-stitch pullovers, Grandma? I've read it.'

. . . Swansea. Oil on the water and ships coming and going and bits of me coming and going with them. A water bird dying with oil in its throat and on its wings . . . Treforest. Barges in the locks carrying coal to Cardiff and later the waterways filling with flowers and the barges falling apart. There was a stone there also that rocked when the wind came down the valley with sadness. And two white towers from a fairy tale . . .

. . . 'There's a man for you, boyo, my brother. He would meet a man on Saturday night, have an argument, and take him home to sleep in the same bed to be sure he would be there for the fight by the Cwm on Sunday morning. Chasing the girls he would be again on Sunday night . . . Oh God, God! In the same pit we were, he working the night of the explosion, me sick and sleeping.'

'Is that brandy, Grandpa?'

'Bang! Up I gets, dust coming down. It's the pit, it's the pit they said. I went to dig him out.'

'Can I taste it, Grandpa?'

'All purple in the face they were and swollen and froth about the mouth. You could not tell one from another.'

'Are you crying, Grandpa?'

'Oh! You two would have been great butties, boyo.'

. . . A day with the heat of summers that are gone and a climb through yellow bursting gorse to the wall of the seminary, and a sneaking through the arrow slits hoping for a chase. But the monks ignored us so we stole some wall-flowers, yellow and brown and some purple. They still ignored us. But then it was very still with everything looking at us so we dropped the flowers and ran.

'Do they take their clothes off ever?' when we stopped.

'No. At one time they did not even piss. Jesus did it for them.'

'That is no favour. I like to piss.'

'Let's have a piss now.'

The sun shone through the drops and we were sorry when we were dry . . .

. . . 'What did Lizzie Lophead want with you?'

'She was only telling me about acts of kindness, Ma. Like not putting a single plate in the oven to warm without putting in another for company. And about when you light a candle you should put it by a mirrored window—and not to forget to blow it out twice.'

'Lizzie Lophead! You leave my boy alone.'

What a laugh Lizzie had!

. . . Was it true? An open-sided hearse, its lamps lit, with a lonely horse pulling and a sodden pile of flowers. Water in the hole that was dug. Did they bury in the dark with men carrying torches and going away in groups. No one speaking—only lies . . .

. . . Holding crusts of bread to swooping seagulls.

'Dad, did-you-ever see that blackbird? When we came to Aber first the blackbirds flapped their wings all the time. The seagulls must have taught them. There's kind the seagulls are. See the black one gliding with the wind?'

'Don't talk foolish.'

. . . And the sea again. Always. Shouting in the dark to a winter wave, things I was afraid to hear . . . With my back to the shore and swearing to swim to the sun and then afraid and going in, and angry you're afraid . . .

Towards evening Morgan went down to the village again and looked at the young girls then went into the *Rose and Crown* for a pint. Two shy men—farmers—tried to speak to him but he hid in the corner and looked at the fire, and the foam patterns in his beer. Before it became crowded he left and walked along the beach. There were lights up the valley and there was white on the sea, but he saw nothing, was aware of nothing.

He picked up three small stones and started towards the *Unicorn* to throw them at the window with the light, but the light seemed too far away. One after the other he threw them into the sea.

CHAPTER NINE

THE DAY was new, was fresh. The sun, red in the haze, was low and large at a gap in the hills. The morning mist had mottled the farm's front, and dew hung on the grass falling from a tumbling wall.

'Pssst!' The boy, with his head out the window, contorted his face, and in silent gesticulation urged Morgan out of the yard. Morgan passed through the gate and walked slowly down the path towards the village. Half-way to the trees Owen caught up with him, and with a shouted 'Run,' ran on, his knees pumping up and down like pistons. In the trees they both slowed to a walk.

'Mam heard me and called out,' Owen said. 'How she knows I do not know but knows she does.'

'Didn't you tell them?' Morgan asked.

'If I told them I couldn't go. They'd watch me.'

'Won't you get the business when you return?'

'Don't let's think about it.' He picked up a stick and did a bit of fencing.

'Looks a good day for fishing,' Morgan said.

'Fishing is better than anything,' said the boy. 'Next after fishing is up at Twm-Shon-the-mole's. But my father likes Twm no more than he likes Will, so I've got to watch out about going there too. They find out everything.'

'How did Twm get his name?'

'You never heard of Twm Shon Catti? He is famous hereabouts. He was a long-time-ago robber who hid his gold in a cave near the bridge. Everyone was scared to go there because of the ghosts. They called Twm-Shon-the-mole after him because he lives not far away and some people think he is spooky. He isn't spooky. Not a bit. And he used to have a mole but now he's got a ferret. I wish my father would let me have a ferret. A ferret and a knife is all I'd ever want. Twm's ferret is called Cyfarthfa.'

By then they were out of the trees. Smoke came up from Will's house and from the *Unicorn*. Owen said, 'I can smell bacon.'

The tide was in as they walked around the quay. The river looked green and there were patches of oil on the harbour water. Boats tied along the wharf and anchored near the harbour mouth tipped to and fro. Owen ran on ahead and rapatapped on the green door, and went in. Morgan followed.

The low-beamed room was dark (windows all to the sea) but flickering with the new firelight. New smoke turned under the mantelpiece as steam rose from a black kettle and fat spat from a black pan.

'Night, night has gone away,' sang out the boy.

'What a day, man and boy,' said Will, scratching his chest all over with both hands. 'Fish are singing, birds are jumping, boats are marvels with little nostrils going oompah.'

'Oompah, oompah,' went Owen.

'Stick it up your jumpah,' Will added. 'Morgan then, did you sleep like a sea-lion?'

'Like a bird. In bed by nine, if you can believe it, and up with the sun.'

'When you're doing nothing, then nothing is the best thing to do,' said Will. 'One thing at a time is all I can manage.'

'This is the day to catch a whopper,' Owen said, wetting a finger to pick up a bread crumb.

'Aye. We are all heroes today,' said Will, 'brave and beautiful.'

The white-scraped table was set with three odd cups, two odd plates and a bowl, a pot of yellow jam, butter in a White Horse whisky ashtray, a big blue teapot and the bread on the boards. The knives had bone handles which had been scorched, and the spoons were of antique shape. The toasting fork was made of brass and shaped like a tree with a devil holding a monkey near the branches which were the prongs.

'Cut the bread, man, and start toasting, boy,' said Will.

Morgan cut thick slices of bread and Owen impaled one on the toasting fork and crouched before the fire. Morgan stuck a fork through another slice and joined him. Will struck a fork against the stove as if for tuning and sang a long deep note before turning the bacon.

'Wonderful, boysbach,' he said, sniffing. 'This will pop your belly button.'

'What a wonder is fire,' said Owen. 'Without it bacon and eggs and mushrooms would be nothing.' Then he dropped the bread into the fire! He jumped up in a flap and bumped against Will who staggered, and fat splashed. Owen jumped again, slapping a hand to his neck. Morgan began to laugh and dropped his slice into the fire.

'Leave it, leave it, boy,' said Will, but Owen had salvaged both pieces and was rubbing them on his sweater, insisting they were good. Vigorously he scraped the toast with a knife, flicking crumbs and cinders all over the room. Will took out the bacon and broke the eggs into the pan, then let it sit on the coals while he poured water into the teapot. The toast, black but buttered, was placed on a stove-top plate to keep warm and more slices were started, the forks propped over the fire.

When the eggs were done the pan was brought to the table and set there for the bread dipping. They sat down and ate. Smoke billowed from the chimney, the toast was gritty and bitter and the eggs greasy, but they ate hungrily and gulped the tea too hot. Will drank from his saucer, in turn blowing on and slurping at the tea.

'I can't stand a breakfast,' he said, 'that's not smoky and smelling and rich and lots of it to take away the taste of sleep. In the morning you've got to review the night—but briefly. Scratch yourself, open your eyes, put in your teeth, take a pee, blow your nose, let out all the gases, hawk and spit a bit, make sure you haven't lost any of your capabilities, and check to see if you've got any new ones. Then—dig in. Fruit and fancy breads for breakfast are for spirit people not for me—gutsy food I need to tell me I'm alive and down to earth again.' As he spoke he stuffed eggs and mushrooms into his mouth, grease dribbling down his chin, his glass eye slipping from side to side as he moved his jaws.

'In the morning,' he went on, 'I want tea so strong you've got to force your spoon into it. Salt and pepper and lots of

132

fat left for the bread. Eight hours up there with the angels is long enough without food.'

'Sometimes I'd like to stay with the angels to see what they do all day,' said Owen.

Will stopped chewing as if in surprise, then dug a spoonful of jam from the pot and slapped it down on Owen's toast. 'All day long is a long time to go without jam, boy,' he said.

Owen laughed and ducked his head to his plate, licking the jam without lifting the toast. Will got up and stuck out his belly and patted it, and wiped his chin. With the large cups reloaded they sat around the fire and made more toast.

'Got a fag?' Will asked, giving his chest an exploratory tap. This time he took only one.

'Let's go,' said Owen.

'Rest a bit,' said Will, scratching a match on the stone floor.

'The fish are waiting.'

'Get the boat ready then,' he said, and the boy went outside with a basket.

Morgan lit up. 'I'm taking off in a couple of days,' he said.

'That soon?'

'It came sudden. I'm missing-out here.'

'Sorry to see you go.'

'I've got to take my finger out and do something.'

'This is something,' Will said, then added quietly, 'Here a man can take fish from the sea, vegetables from the earth, firewood from the seashore and flowers from the hill.'

'It's not for me.'

'Then just stay for a couple more drunks. You don't get brew like that in America.'

Morgan took a gulp of tea and put his feet up on a mouse-torn footstool. 'That was a good night at the *Rose and Crown*.'

'It's always like that,' Will said. 'They're just a bunch of armpits.'

'I'll miss them. Where I come from the bars are so dark you could have a babe's boobs out on the table and the guy next to you wouldn't know.'

'Aye? But is that the place to go after boobs?'

'Barmen are like pimps where I come from.'

'It is not better than the grass, I bet,' Will said. But he was just talking out of his memories, not hinting.

'Not better than the grass,' he said again. 'You know, I am not much of a seaman. I have been on land for years. The smell of cowshit I like as much as I do the smell of seaweed. The sea is not for me. Was not even when I was a boy—weeks and weeks at sea and then was port with all the bed faggots diseased. Fucksome but diseased. I like it here. I've got a woman and a fire and a roof and a boat. What more! The good thing about the sea is that when a man comes back from it people hope but do not expect him to settle down and be respectable. They expect to be shocked and although too old I have grown to want to shock people, I like the feeling that I don't have to wonder whether they will like my actions or not. Too old I am to revolt so glad I am I've got the reputation.'

'With no reputation it's better in the city,' Morgan said.

'Like three rebels we are then, with you and me and Owen. But only Owen is the true rebel and he doesn't see himself as one.'

'We try too hard.'

'We do. As men we should be more like my brother.

He's got something somewhere.' He tapped his head and then his chest. 'He says to me, does Caradoc, "Willie, you and I have jobs that are like symbols, that must be it. People see you only as good and you are affected by what they see —what else could it be why someone so wicked is so happy." Not for you, Morgan, but for us this place is right. Dead it is sometimes like a cut-off dick but for me a good place to live. People are as bad as in any other place. No worse. Backward they are and stubborn but sometimes they trust the day ahead—some do.'

'When are we going, Willie?' Owen asked from the doorway.

'Now,' he said, jumping up. A gulp of tea and a dash of dregs into the fire and they left, leaving the hissing fire and the empty cups and the dirty plates.

The boat was small like a rowboat, white with an autumn-red sail hanging limp. Her name was *Daisy*. There were two plank seats and a tarpaulin-covered box in the bow.

Will fixed the oars and, standing, edged the boat into the river current.

Morgan, stumbling up front, said, 'Just keep the crate level, man, that's all I ask. When I put my fanny down I want to know it's going to hit something solid.'

'Willie, put your eye on the prow so it'll look after us,' Owen said.

'No fear,' said Will. 'It's got to see me through the week.'

A seagull called. The village was empty, with no sound. The pure water, reluctant, like ice, to move away behind; a cool air came from it. Rollocks, rattling, echoed. It was still early. . . .

'I haven't been on a boat for twenty years,' Morgan said.

Owen rolled his eyes. 'My father doesn't go fishing and he is miserable all the time.'

'Some people are miserable whatever they do,' Morgan said . . . but guilt was not entirely absent.

'The only time your old man is not miserable,' said Will, 'is when he is warming your backside. A great time he will have when he finds you have been with me—and on a Sunday too.'

It did not look like a Sunday.

The stone quay had slipped by and the river's flow had lost its thrust.

'From the sea, Wales looks like a hundred buxom women flat on their backs,' Will said.

The sea was in a slow swell, and when the wind came it was fitful, but the sail snapped and filled, and the boat heeled and water bubbled beneath the bow. The oars were shipped and the tiller was fitted.

'The wind will stay the day, I think,' said Will, 'though perhaps we will have to row a bit if we are afraid of the dark.'

'Just the day to find a sea-serpent,' said Owen.

'Where are we going, Captain?' Morgan asked him, knowing it wasn't asked well.

'Atlantis,' Owen said, but only after a pause.

'Are you armed?'

'We don't need arms,' said Owen, still not sure.

'I've never been there,' said Morgan.

'I bet you have—if you ever dream. It is a place like King Arthur's country. Knights and giants and dwarfs and beetles and dragons and birds and reptiles and pools with goldfish.'

'All under the sea?'

136

'All under the sea.'

'Don't they get water up their noses?'

Owen watched him for a moment then said, 'No,' and bent to pick at his scabby knees.

Three seagulls flapped low on labouring wings, calling out as if in pain.

'Seagulls are the lost souls of seamen,' Will said, and straight away Owen brightened. He rummaged through the box of food and came up with an apple and a slab of fruit-cake; these he placed on the seat before moving back to where Will was leaning on the rudder bar, and putting his hand into Will's trouser pocket.

'Suck in your stomach, Willie,' he said. Willie did so and Owen took out a knife. 'This is the kind of knife I want when I am independent,' he added. He rubbed it on his chest, then took a fish from under the seat and started to cut slivers of flesh from it.

'Have a beer,' Will said. Morgan looked at his watch. 'Don't see if it is time, fellow. Test your tongue, tap the roof of your mouth.'

'All I've done here is eat and drink,' Morgan said. He opened a flagon and passed it to Will who took a swig and handed it back. Owen baited a hook and dropped the line, then bit hugely at the cake.

'When you finish drinking, let's send a message in the bottle,' Owen said.

'No,' said Will, 'there's tuppence on it.'

They were sailing north and the boom was out, the wind holding the boat over. The boat dipped and there was some roll and sometimes the water hissed close to the topside, a deep, crackled-green-glass water with a turning darkness below. A moving, swelling, fertile sea. Rich with all wonders. Owen talked about the everlasting churn in Cardigan Bay which, night and day, churned out salt. When the tale was told he bent from the bow and dipped his hand into the frothing water and scooped some to his mouth. It went spluttering out.

'It is getting saltier,' he said. 'Definitely.'

'Boyo, you will never learn,' Will said. 'The sea is like a woman. Looks good but not always so tasty.'

'Tastes horrible.'

'Wash your mouth out with beer,' Will said. The boy clambered to the stern and carefully held the bottle in both hands, blinking against the sun as he lifted it. He made a face.

'Almost as bad as the sea,' he said.

'Now you are going crackers,' exclaimed Will.

'A lake would be a better place to fish,' said Owen.

'Fresh water,' said Will to Morgan, 'welcomes you like a woman but the sea tolerates you like a mistress. That is why I ran away to sea. Look at it. No liberties can you take with the sea. Here we have an innocent day but it cannot stay respectable long.'

'What is that line up ahead going out to sea?' Morgan asked.

'It is the Roman road,' Will said. 'When the legions were here all this was a plain behind a bloody great dyke. Sixteen fortified cities and a fertile plain. All lost because a man could not hold his drink.'

'My sister has heard the sunken bell ring out,' said Owen. 'My father says my sister is cracked.'

'Your father thinks everyone is cracked,' said Will. 'You know what? If you ask me he is the only one around here who is cracked.'

Owen laughed. 'My father says that nothing you say is of any importance. He says that you are going to hell as sure as fish is fish.'

'As long as I don't meet him there,' Will grumbled.

Owen, pointing at the line ahead, said, 'That is where little men like blacksmiths come on summer nights in cockleshell boats and invade us. They don't do much harm though.'

Four white horses sped up the road from the sea and disappeared among the rocks leaving wisps of water-smoke behind them. Will leaned out on the rudder bar and the boat went over the turbulent water: bouncing and twisting but still on swiftly, froth bursting, sea boiling—hot lava caught in a wintry sea. Owen stood, legs bent to meet the dancing of the boat, waving his arms at the water and shouting as if at an army. Then they were through the rough, turning away from the shore and out into the open. Far out, almost over the edge of the world, was a white sail, lonely-looking and lovely like a bird entering a cloud.

'Sailors like to think of the sea only as a surface and with no depth,' said Will. 'Daft are sailors sometimes.'

The boat dipped into a trough and a splash came aboard.

'In the past,' Will said, 'children were conceived by things like that—by the contact of raindrops and seaspray and even seagull droppings. Sometimes just by turning your arse to the wind.'

'Not a very happy state of affairs,' said Morgan.

A jelly-fish sailed by, its toadstool back creased in green and purple patterns, its limp but curled tendrils hanging down, waiting.

'All the things I have seen in the oceans,' said Will, his mouth full of bread and cheese. 'Some things like hippopotopotomusses, some things like swallows, some like snakes, some bigger than houses, brighter than blushes, smaller than tadpoles; some like harpies, some like devils, some that taste like butter, some that sting like sin . . . There is variety true enough in the world. Like women. You'd think that they would be similar, what with all their goodies having to be in the usual places, but all the endless varieties! Black and shiny ones, white and pimply ones, some with flesh so just the right kind to look at or to touch. Little timid pudding dumplings and big bold ones who look at you with such a relish that makes you wonder maybe they would rather chop you up for stew. Women with rubies in their noses, or diamonds on their brows, with flowers in their hair or rings through their ears. Some in black like blackbirds with festering eyes, some like peacocks. Covered in sheets or sheaths of grass with ohsosmooth and bare—boyo,' to Owen, 'when you get to be a man go you to the islands.'

'Talk about the animals,' said Owen.

'You've got to see the world, boy, you have to go all over. I've seen it all and of all I've seen it's half I do believe. Cities on hills with marble streets and fancy bands, dancing girls, coloured lanterns, golden temples, silver gongs, whizz-bangs in the sky and processions through the streets and carnivals and circuses . . .'

'With elephants?' Cake crumbling from his mouth.

'Elephants and falling clowns and tigers and shaggy lions, big brown bears, dancing dogs, fine white horses, applauding seals. Strong men in leopard skins and ladies on swings and acrobats and top-hatted men with now-you-see-it-now-you-don't. A circus is like a world—sometimes.'

Will took out his teeth and held them over the side to

clean them. The ruffled water round his hand was like a family of silver mice.

'But say again about the animals.'

Will put his teeth back in. 'You know more about animals than I do. If I was whoever invents animals I couldn't think up half of them. I couldn't have dreamed up a kangaroo, or a giraffe if I was fed on rum for thirty years. Or an ostrich or a pelican. I like them now I've seen them. They're a damn sight prettier than people, many of them. And there are only a few things you've got to go on when you make a beast—head, neck, body, arms, legs, wings, tail—that's all. Everything's been tried.'

Owen said, 'I could make up a new one. It would be a small animal covered in white fur with a head like a mushroom, and his eyes would have patterns in them and would change colour every second and sparkle like the kali-tube you look through . . .'

Talk goes on and covers many matters, but sometimes, Morgan realized, there are moments of quiet and in those moments each is within himself looking out at the world as if through a pinhole pierced in tissue paper, the paper colouring the edges of the image: each secure behind his peephole, with face relaxed. It is like a film with no sound-track, and with a camera turning without haste on all the contiguous things, oblivious to plot and to the order of importance of objects. All objects being given the chance to prove their place. The camera waits with uncritical eye, and the objects perform or move or stay there in the sun or with their own light, and take on beauty. Images grow in permanence, are put away as treasures . . .

. . . The grain of wood, weather-ridged, under a brown, firm hand.

. . . Three green empty bottles and an unfleshed fish in a bed of tangled line.

. . . The edge of the sea tipping to and fro, the sky with it.

. . . The boy, now still, his cheek against the wood, one hand in the water the other cupped over his ear regulating the sound of the sea, relegating it, playing tunes on it, his mouth open, listening; his hair being lifted and turned in the wind.

. . . The sail taut but with an occasional undulation as if a woman undressed behind it.

. . . A cormorant, up from diving, its long clerical neck jerking down the fish.

There is only so much the eye can take in, and again like the camera as it moves, there builds up an almost unbearable tension as to what it will focus on next. It is like being aware of the presence of some horror, and the hero goes through the castle, his eye the camera—along corridors, down staircases, past statues, silently around the hall, in between and about unfamiliar furniture, not yet near it, no it isn't there, nor there yet, no it isn't there, no—yes oh my god yes . . ! And the same it is with beauty. Slowly the eye moves and the response comes, no, no, to everything, but the apprehension is mounting, and then yes oh my god yes when the next is beauty. Oh there is fear all right in beauty. Sometimes as if in horror the eyes are averted, coming back only to make sure. But not staying.

The fish they caught were small and did not fight much but they twisted and shone as they came up through the water. They died in stiff arcs and in red, red blood. Despite the water thrown on them the red remained.

'Mackerel should not be so pretty, or should not taste so

good,' Owen said, looking at Will, but getting no answer.

In the afternoon with the wind freshening and turning to the south, Will tacked the boat, not gaining much but edging towards home. The colour of the day had changed. To the north the light from the lighthouse came on, blinking on and off as it swung round. Morgan put his hands in the water, rubbing them together and keeping them beneath the surface, looking at them in the water that had turned black, cleaning them, chilling them. His scalp tingled and his eyes smarted: he tasted salt on his lips.

Then the rocket burst. To the south, clear, the spark slowly falling.

Owen whooped.

'What's that?' Morgan asked.

'Distress signal,' said Will, jumping for the sail.

The second flare went up.

'What could happen on a day like this?'

'An engine bust and no sail maybe,' Will said. 'Drifting on the rocks.'

'Hurry,' said Owen. 'Let's help with the lifeboat.'

Two short tacks and the boat was heading for the harbour entrance. A man in a yellow slicker and a bowler hat clanged away at a bell on the wharf. The day was almost gone and the village lights were on but dim. Through the streets a crowd of men came pulling the lifeboat carriage to the slipway.

Inside the harbour the wind died and Will scrambled for the oars. 'Wait for me,' he shouted. 'I'm the bosun.' The lifeboat carriage was against the head of the slipway, and the pullropes were being laid aside. Men were getting aboard.

The moment Will's boat bumped against the wharf he

143

and Owen were out and running. By the time Morgan had tied up, Will was in the lifeboat pulling on oilskins.

The last ropes were shaken loose. Men stood back. With a rush and a smack and a sway the lifeboat was down the slipway into the water, and was away with a roar from its engines. Small boats bobbed in the wash, and waves slopped against the wharf before echoing back across the harbour, rippling the pale lines of lantern light. Small night seabirds altogether went once over the harbour before settling on the rocks, with no voice.

The watching people were in two groups like weights around the fulcrum of the empty lifeboat carriage. In one the men stiff and tidy in their Sunday suits and the women in their Sunday coats and bits of fur: in the other, all men in caps and mufflers. Both groups silent, the one still like a waiting choir, the other busy coiling ropes and fitting capstan bars and turning round the carriage. One woman in the chapel-waiting group held the bowler hat and stiff collar of her man who was in the boat.

Washed-up seaweed popped underfoot as Morgan walked towards the slipway. The boat was almost out of sight now, way beyond the wharf; the waves were now higher and the lifeboat dipped and was sometimes lost, its red light appearing only intermittently.

Morgan rolled down his shirt sleeves and put on his jacket more against the darkness than the chill. Little emotion showed on the faces of the people in the crowd for nothing to fear was seen in the evening. With no sign of storm this was merely something to relieve the monotony of an abstemious Welsh Sunday. But with some, their lives were the sea, their pleasures by day, their duty by night. When the challenge came each knew his place.

144

Morgan put a cigarette between his lips, and, finding no match, he went up to an old man leaning against the capstan. He asked for a light and offered the pack. The old man interrupted his mournful between-the-teeth whistle to accept the smoke. He struck the match with his thumbnail; the flare of the match lit up his dim eyes and made the air dark about them.

'Does this happen often?' Morgan asked.

'Three or four times a year.' The cigarette danced up and down.

'Do people die out there?'

'Not often. But some do.' With the cigarette dangling the whistling started up again.

The work around the capstan was done and the men, sharing tobacco, settled down to wait, some sitting on the shafts of the carriage, some on their heels hugging their knees, the glow from their smokes coming and going. The other group began to break up, the people climbing the hill like straggling black sheep, children hanging back on straight arms twisting to look for the long-gone boat. Mrs Pritchard was there, huddled in her wheelchair and clutching a shawl about her, but she made no move to leave.

'Dearo-dearo-dearo,' she said over and over, shaking her head, but her eyes were bright and she slipped her tongue in and out like a satisfied cat. Behind her, going up and down in his squeaking Sunday shoes, was Mr Pritchard, turning his black square hat against his chest and avoiding Morgan's look.

Someone came down the hill through the chapel-goers and Morgan, not sure but hopeful, walked to the bottom of the hill. When he was sure he went to meet her. He touched her hand but did not take it, then together they came and stood at the edge of the wharf between the two groups.

'Is Will in the boat?' Gwylan asked.

'Yes.'

'He has not missed one yet.'

The waves were white-topped now, and though the wind was not much stronger the air felt heavy with spray.

'There's fine they are,' she said. 'Sometimes it is so rough they can hardly leave the harbour, yet they always respond. From the hill sometimes you can see them when they put on their searchlight.'

'Would you like to go up the hill?'

'Not now.'

The day had gone from Dyfnaint but over the lowest inch of sky the day hung on into the night like fire from a black sun.

'Mr Johns!' It was Parry, calling before he got close, leading Owen by an ear. Parry, dark faced, glared at Gwylan who turned away with pursed lips.

'Yes?' With displeasure.

'Aware you must be of my instructions to Owen about not going fishing with,' he lowered his voice, 'Will Williams. You heard me this very morning yesterday. Yet you took him fishing.'

'I didn't take him any place. We were both guests on the same boat,' he said, with a smile at Owen.

'You encouraged him in his flouting of authority.'

'I can't say what scene or can or can't make,' he said.

Parry moved his hold to the hair and wagged Owen's head back and forth. 'Too much meddling in my affairs there is, Mr Johns. You do not seem to appreciate my good sense.'

146

'Lower the spray, man—this shirt ain't drip-dry.'

'I do not like your attitude.'

Morgan sighed. 'So few people do.'

'It must be made clear that I am the master in my house and you must abide by the rules of my house . . .'

'Depends on the rules.'

'I make the rules and with no interference. I say who the members of my household see and what they do. I forbid you from now on to go anywhere with this boy. Do you understand please.'

'Lower, man, lower—you'll put the old drums out of tune. Anyway . . .'

'I am telling you quietly,' Parry shouted. 'I am not a man to be meddled with.'

'Seems to me you were meddled with by someone who didn't know what he was doing.' He laughed. 'Anyway— as I was about to say—I'll be digging out the day after tomorrow.'

'Good,' said Parry. He tugged away at Owen's hair as he turned. Owen said, 'Let me get my fish . . .' but it ended in 'Ow!' as, head wagging, he was guided up the hill.

'I see you did not get to the lifeboat in time, Mr Parry,' Gwylan shouted after him.

Parry stopped for a last blast. 'They never rescue anyone. By the time it takes them to pull that old boat through the streets a whole fleet could sink.'

'Owen's got a big job there,' Morgan said to Gwylan. 'If he wants to stay frisky.'

'Is it true?' she asked. 'You have only one more full day in Dyfnaint?'

'Yes.'

'I am sorry.'

'Do you have to go back to the *Unicorn* tonight?'

'I won't,' she said.

'Then help me unload Will's boat.'

They took some of the fish to Maggie's ice-box and Maggie gave them a secret nip. From the bar they could hear a faint hymn—the prelude to the sermon on the Ways of the Wicked.

★   ★   ★   ★   ★

Will's room at night was like a cave with cobweb stalactites and with flames fluttering in the draught from the wall crevices. Dark, but secure with everything that was needed somewhere close at hand.

And with no clock. 'What would Will do with a clock,' Gwylan said. 'He does nothing but wait for the day, and then for the moon.'

A muffled knocking sounded outside. 'It is his boat,' she said, 'on a length of rope like a horse. You ought to know, you tethered it there.'

Insistent is the knocking. 'It is no more than the river current,' she said.

And sometimes the boat came tapping at the door as the lighthouse light came sweeping past the window so that the beam had a taptap to it. The sea, clock-like, beat and rushed, turning back after a pause with a sucking away at the pebbles. All the noise was outside.

A white mouse came out from behind a cupboard—hello mouse—and nosed around under the table. Finding something it sat up and nibbled, moved on, tail snaking, found something and sat up and so on. Then whiskers twitched—

148

don't go, mouse—but it was on its way, neck-stretched tail-straight, back to its hole.

'Now we have all eaten,' Morgan said.

'It had ruby eyes,' said Gwylan.

'Will's lefty's like a pearl,' he said. 'He should set it in a ring and give it to Mrs Pritchard.'

'His good one is sparkling right now. They never get there first but the try is worth a blow-out.'

'He'll need a nip when he gets back.'

'Would you like another?'

He shook his head. He had eaten, he had drunk.

'Would you like a bath?' she asked. 'You look tired.'

'You mean I look dirty.'

'It would do you good,' she said.

'In some black back shed with the wind whistling?'

'Before the fire.'

'Yeah?' He nodded, thinking it unlikely to happen but happy in the thought that it might.

She showed him how. A tin tub like a chariot was taken from its outside nail and placed before the fire. Green-painted outside, white-painted inside. Two buckets of cold water went into it, then a full bucket and kettle were hung on the fire hooks. Then she and he sat tight together in the deep chair to wait.

Morgan put a cigarette between her lips and took one himself. Gwylan twisted a paper spill and lit it from the fire. After she touched the cigarettes he took the spill from her and held it like a torch between them . . . There should be rubies there against your throat: red like a mouse's eye, red like ashes, red like souls. A string of rubies against your throat to count like prayerbeads—red like tongues, like birds . . . but he did not say a word.

149

The spill burnt almost to his fingers before he threw it in the fire. The burnt-out form rose on the air like a floating city with the lights on and went up the chimney.

He was tired. The day had been long and the places far apart, but the tiredness did not demand sleep. His arm about her, his hand not holding her, her hair a breath away, her ear uncovered in sweet convolution, her cheek like that of an apple. 'Sometimes you cannot be sure of your own dimensions,' she said. And she was right. Her shoulder against his chest, thigh against thigh, here her wrist, there his hand. Where does flesh of one end, the other begin?

Desire was dormant, yet the touch was warm and kind as when you lean over a child to tug on his swimsuit and his eager joy is transmitted through his shoulders.

Time passed.

Morgan took a nub-end drag then threw the butt into the fire and she threw hers after it. When wisps of steam came from the lidded bucket and a song came from the kettle she got up.

'At the *Unicorn* we have a noisy copper geyser,' she said, 'which isn't half as fine.'

'I've always thought of cleanliness as a function rather than a ritual.'

'Ritual has such a bad name now,' she said, smiling. She dragged the tub closer to the fire and shielded it from the draught with two chairs and a blanket between, then placed soap in a saucer and a towel on the fire fender. Morgan poured some of the boiling water into the tub. With a dropping of her hands and an inclining of the head she indicated the bath was ready.

She waited, hands bent under on hips like a washer-woman, but as soon as he unbuttoned his shirt she turned and went outside—for more water, she said. He kept on his pants while he poured from the hot and the cold until the water was comfortable ('what's right for the elbow's seldom right for the bum,' . . . back there, there must have been another old aunty somewhere) then he unzipped and dropped them, and was in in a splash. When she returned he had frothed up with soap and had floated the washcloth where the pink tip of his pecker bobbed up and down in the soapsuds.

'Come on in, the water's fine,' he said, splashing about him.

'You need more sun,' she said, pressing a thumb against his pink arms and examining the white mark it left. 'Part of you looks like a dogfish and part looks like a kipper.'

'Baste me a bit.'

She cupped water over him then soaped the brush and went to work on his back.

'Stop when you strike blood,' he said.

'How do unmarried men ever get their backs clean?' she asked.

'If it's a big job we call in friends and serve beer. What do unmarried women do?'

'Contortion's the answer,' she said.

She finished scrubbing and floated the brush like a boat, then went to the fireside chair and sat with her legs under her, watching him. Morgan slid down till he could rest with his head on the headboard of the tub; his knees stuck up like scuttled ships, his legs patterned in seaweed hair.

Abruptly, she said, 'What made you give up?'

'Uh? Oh! The question should be what made me come here in the first place.'

'But now you're here—why go?'

'I always feel guilty when I enjoy myself,' he said. She did not answer and there were no words while he soaked himself. When he made to get up she came and stood behind him, and when he got up she poured fresh water over him to rinse away the suds. After he had dried himself and dressed they emptied the tub, and then she brought him beer, and they sat together before the fire.

'Couldn't Howell Powell help you?' she asked.

'He'll probably find something but I can't wait. Say he's alive. We sit down, have a beer. How y'been? OK. That's good. Great times back there. Yeah. Shake your head over things that never happened—over made-up stories.'

'That would be nice.'

'His world would have stopped fifty years back.'

'What is fifty years?'

'It's a lot to me,' he said.

'Time goes so wonderfully slow. Nothing big happens quickly.'

'Fifty years!' he said. 'Things have come like nothing there was before. Words have new sounds to them, music another bang, all the crazy machines. With all this, people have to be different.'

'Some are, even here.'

'Maybe there are places where change is only a different side of things but where I've been it's something new you've got to look at for your own peace of mind. They ask what's the point of living now if all your praise is for the past. Now is the time they suck in air, now's the time you're sick. I guess this is why I'm leaving. What would Rhydderch know of what I'm saying. Even you don't.'

She laughed, low-voiced.

'The past is gone,' he said. 'That's what you build the future on—that's all. Don't go back.'

'Who's disagreeing?' she said, her laughter still close. But he went on, not insistent, but getting it out.

'This old man and I—if we met—we each would not want to see the other's side. He'd be stodgy, I'd be stubborn. What's he going to say to me? Keep your nose clean, don't drink on an empty stomach, believe in God, for Christ's sake?' He took a drink of beer. 'I know the way that's right with me. I get crisp and green enough to keep me in beer and bologni and that's always been my taste. My old man said Grando would set me straight. How did my old man know what straight was! The world changes—what would he know of my world?'

'What would your world be like if you had your way?' she asked.

'Like the one I miss right now . . . ("What is conviction anyway, man? It ain't the tone of your horn—there's always spooks") . . . but with more sparkle, with me not missing what's doing. Like I don't want to get involved in the world with me feeling in my belly every wrangle and fight and fear, and joining things, and pledging, and up in the morning and all that responsibility jazz where the world's problems are mine, but . . .' He took a gulp of beer to let time intrude, for who wants to end a sentence like that. 'My place is where guys are always pushing against the boundaries of experience. Does that sound fairy to you? It's always like that! When you try to put your thoughts into words they come out pompous or queer. All you mean is a little thing and out it comes like tubas.'

Her head was resting on his shoulder, but her face was

turned away. 'Say something,' he said. But she made no
sound and did not move.

After a while he said, 'It isn't right to scratch in the sand
to see how things used to be. Like when I leave here how
will I see you? You'll be more lovely, more exciting than
could be possible. So say some day I come back and I take
a look and I say that's it. You'd be even more lovely but
you'd have to be less than what I remembered. Everyone
builds monuments in their minds, but they're not made
with any materials that I know, that's for sure.'

'Do you believe all you say?' she said.

'I don't know. Sometimes I just don't listen.'

'Sometimes I think there is only one world and that is
inside me. All the rest is scenery.'

'Whoop-de-doo!'

'What does that mean?'

'All this inner drunkenness! It's the weakness of the
Welsh.'

'And their strength?'

'Maybe,' he said.

She got up and sat on a corner of his chair and put her
arms about him, her body like powerful hands.

'Two days side by side,' she said. 'In one of them all the
fears are there and I go around with that sick feeling. All
worry, and then today—wonder. Still sorry you are leaving
but happy inside.' With her lips she pinched the corners of
his mouth, the words vibrating against his cheek. 'I'm happy
you came,' she said. 'Dyfnaint is no longer the world. Now
I can look over the hedge. Perhaps one day I will look for
a gate. But glad I am that I did not try to find it before I
knew the full extent of this place.'

'If you move on—any place—before you get what you

came for,' Morgan said, 'it's easy to say it's the impatience of a youth you somehow think you missed. It's better to stay and know it, I guess, but if you keep moving you can almost convince yourself you're looking.'

Gwylan said nothing.

'In a similar way,' he went on, 'without working at it, you can play the hunch that somehow you're going to leave your mark, you're going to do something pretty damn good. As long as you don't have to work at it.'

'My uncle is a poet,' Gwylan said, 'and he watches trains go by. There is a blacksmith in the village who plays the harp: Will says that he is not a good blacksmith but he plays a lovely harp.'

'I know. I hate to think that contributes anything. The real sad ones are those who don't know how high they can get. Always there's a higher judge. Accomplishment is always a day away ... But you know, a lot of guys—they've got their problems—and sometimes they work on them, trying to use what they've got with what's all around. Trying to know what makes them act like bastards. They work so hard at it they end up unable to tie a shoelace—unless the shoe is on someone else's foot ...' But Gwylan blubbered his lips.

'I wasn't listening again,' he said. 'What was it all about?'

'Whatever it was, it's yours.' She turned up her head and time passed.

'When I get back,' he said, 'I'll get me a place with a fireplace and I'll buy me a tub so if ever you're in town look me up and I'll pay you back.'

'I'd like that,' she said.

They heard the motor of the returning lifeboat, but

neither moved. Later they heard Will coming home. He sang loudly and kicked his feet at the pebbles, and when he came in it was like an explosion.

'We got 'em, we got 'em,' he shouted. 'First time in twelve years we got there first. A man and a boy, and the boat shipping water and almost on the rocks—Christ!' He stamped quickly with each foot and laughed. ' "Jump," says Ned to the dumb buggers but they hung on and the waves chopping over the boat. Then the boy jumped and in he came, but his old man, the fool, just shook his head. Every-one shouting jump jump then the boat tipping away and jump he did—right into the bloody sea. Down he went and the boats clashed together and we thought he'd had it for sure, but when the boats wash apart, up he comes spout-ing like a barrel, so I reaches over and grabs him by the moustache.' Will bent over in laughter.

'Have a cup of tea, Will,' said Gwylan, laughing too.

'Tea! Tea! Is that all you've got for a bloody hero? I reaches down, grabs his moustache and yanks him up. His upper lip comes away like a sow's belly but we got him in all right. And just as we got him aboard, the Newquay lifeboat came up like a storm.' He plopped down and pulled at his wet shoes but went on talking.

' "Well, mun," said I to Moustache, "did you see the angels?" Moustache nodded away as if in chapel, "I thought I was done-for that time," he said. There he was, his eyes popping and the bloody big goobers hanging.'

'Goobers? I thought goobers were peanuts?' said Morgan.

'Goobers! Goobers! Goobers is the snot that hangs from your nose when you come back from the dead.'

'Let's go, Morgan,' Gwylan said. 'Will, you are spoiling our mood.'

156

'I'm not spoiling mine. God! It was a good night. Twelve years it has been for us.'

Morgan offered Will a cigarette then got up to go. 'I'll see you before I leave,' he said.

Will became serious. 'Tomorrow I am going up to see Twm-the-mole. You and Gwylan come.'

Morgan and Gwylan looked at each other. 'For a while,' she said, and Morgan nodded.

'Good,' said Will. 'What a rescue! Boyo, there is a moral for you—always keep your manly whiskers, for you never know when they will come in handy.'

They left him then.

The stars were out like children, and small clouds there were like kites.

The lifeboat was at the bottom of the slipway, but the rope was already around the drum. Men, hitching their trousers, putting out smokes, spitting on their hands, were taking their places three to a capstan bar. The dim-eyed man with whom Morgan had shared a smoke coughed and spat, then called 'Roll around, boys, roll around,' and off they jogged around the drum, jumping when they came to the taut rope. 'Hup-anarara-and-a-hup,' went the call as around and around they ran. Slowly the lifeboat was drawn up the slipway, to the sounds of the clanking of the capstan pegs, the clatter of boots, and the singing call.

Morgan stopped and watched, his good feeling gone again. Someone has to face the storm, has to fear, fire the flare, and someone has to put out after them. And someone, he knew, always has to wait, womanlike, for the boat to return. But was it always the same people?

'What is it?' Gwylan asked.

'Whatever it is, it's mine,' he answered, but not rudely.

The village was settling down again after the excitement; houses, one after the other, went into darkness. Street lamps lowered under the brightness of the sky.

On the way back to Gwylan's place, Morgan said, looking up, 'I didn't know Wales could be like this.'

'It is for you, Morgan,' she said. 'Do not forget it.'

* * * * *

That night Morgan found a note from Mair Parry on his pillow. It read: 'My father tells me that you are leaving in a day, and about this I am sorry. It is not right for you to leave thinking that we are sinful people. Tomorrow will be a pretty day, so if you can get up at five o'clock you may come with me, and I will show you what it is. But please be quiet.'

It could have brought up a smile, but it did not. Somewhere the night was swinging, but here was the night for blues: sadness and joy lay side by side, but sadness was the dominant.

The smell of tallow hung in the air, long after the candle was blown, thickening the dead smell of the room.

CHAPTER TEN

A LITTLE man with a smile rather malicious sometimes comes in the night when you awaken with no tingaling. He comes astride a black goat who eats everything (his bell tinkles as he chews). The little man looks the kind of guy you feel fine with, the kind who likes his oats regular and a nip regular, and although he's got wings it's maybe just to get around better. That halo, if that's what it is, could be made of brass, for there's plenty of that about him. He comes without knocking in the middle of the night when your eyes goddamn are wide open, and you're not too keen to get back to the round and round of dreams. 'Three wishes,' he says like a cockney-chinaman selling dirty postcards. 'You want three wishes? Oh blimey! Sublimey!' What the hell, why not—you can't sleep and you can't get up in the dark. Take money for the first wish. (The little man almost chuckles.) Go ahead and spend it. A million million green-eyed presidencies. Spend them.

Sit up! Sit up! At last a kind God! What an opportunity for a man who would be great. A million million crispies. THOU SHALT NOT BE UNHAPPY!

DECREES and ORDERS fly like sparklers. CLEAN UP the sores, and HIDE AWAY the sick; BEFATHER and BEMOTHER the ragged children who offend us with their crying and with their enormous eyes; Oh peace on earth ('for what it's worth'); EDUCATE; PUBLISH masterpieces, COLLECT miracles: BUILD a city—anonymously ('Just a simple statue with a good like-ness in some small-but-beautiful, out-of-the-way square, with perhaps some lights at night'). Keep poor poets, be humane to the old, give-unto-death the beggars, treat art lovers to what is good. Build images, sell souls. Change them—build my wall higher . . . There'd be automobiles with Monday, Tuesday, Wednesday on them in old-gold uncial, a waterfall in the library, goldfish in the toilet. A golden space-filler fills a space and when there are no more spaces then build another place with more built-in spaces. Accumulate and clutter up the vision; project a moving picture on the window of your soul . . . And then, smack smack and dribble—hot and cold running babes in each room, in twoses and threeses, dressed like this, undressed like that, proficient in this, insatiable in this—wow! that's all . . . But we would not neglect the spiritual, oh no. There would be a room with a *tatami* on the floor and *shojis* against the light and a single graceful vase with a few leaves —we could have a little man come in a couple of days a week to change the arrangement—and simple robes and we could sit there and contemplate and improve ourselves. Just you and me. Who's you? Am I not alone? No, man, no man is ever alone with the magic three wishes . . . Worry away, oh worry away the darkness until you are tied up tight in bedclothes spending a million bucks a year . . . 'Two more wishes, mister. Queer mother? Patient sister?'

If you are wise you'd wish, before it's too late, for the little man's brother. He's the one in the yellow combinations and a painted red rose and a big, big daisy growing from his bowler hat, and his flap is down and his fly hangs open and there's a red ribbon round his dingie. He don't have no wishes, only smiling gestures (he got no tongue, poor fellow) and small plans. You're not so much at ease with him though, despite his smile. Yet, come to think of it, he's a much finer fellow altogether. But he comes along at a different time . . .

Morgan checked the time as if he didn't know: five to five. Bedtime back home with the horns still wet. He pulled the clothes back around his head. Mornings were the worst —at the best of times. Confidence gets up later.

Outside he heard the whining of a pleased dog.

The sky was black with no hint of day; the air was chill and damp. Shut your peepers, he mumbled, you need the rest. It's just to watch the sun come up. But it was no use.

He got up and dressed. He passed through the room with the troubled sleepers and tiptoed down the stairs. Quietly he closed the outside door.

Mair and the two dogs were on the hill, against the sky. He turned up the collar of his coat and started up the hill. The cigarette he'd taken he did not light until he came close to her. In the flare of the match her eyes were wide and there was an excited, maybe frightened, look in them. One of the dogs nuzzled his legs and he grunted at it but fondled its ear. He sucked a lungful of smoke and blew it out; it hung like mist.

'Sure it's worth it?' he asked.

'Not sure for you.'

'You couldn't just tell me?'

'It wouldn't be the same.'

'You know I was only teasing you?'

'But there was truth in it for you,' she said.

'Just a joke,' he said.

'This is the first time I have ever disobeyed my father,' she said.

'It's too early in the morning to be sinning.'

'He told me not to be alone with you again.'

'What does he think I'll do—drag you off into the bushes?' He put out a hand and grasped her hair. It was soft, and wet with dew. Perhaps she had waited an hour. His voice became gentle.

'Don't you think it might be good to disobey when you know you have done no wrong?'

'No,' she answered.

She bent to the dogs and whispered 'Go home', and when they'd gone, they walked over the hill away from the house.

As they walked a silence descended like a furry beast. No sound from the sea. No wind, no birds. The murmur from the falls was without variation and was soft. The only other sound was the swish as their feet went through the wet grass. A faint light was now over the mountains: the beginning of a clear day. Morgan finished his cigarette and flicked the stub in the air before them, the end glowing in an arc.

'What you're doing is important, isn't it?' Morgan said.

'You won't tell him, will you?' she said.

'No. We don't have much to say to each other.'

'I know. I am not sure whether or not it has been good having you in the house, Mr Johns. I have hardly seen you

162

and we have not talked much yet—sometimes you shock me.'

'You shock easily.'

'But things happen.'

'Like what?'

'My father is on edge, my mother also. You make them feel they have done something bad.'

'I exist, is that it?'

'I do not know how it is, but—if you'll pardon—it is not easy to put a finger on, but—the way you talk as relaxed as if no one is in the room watching, no respect for what should be respected.'

'I act as I am, Mair. You think there's disrespect?'

'But to my father.'

'This isn't it at all, is it? It's something else.'

'I am sure I do not know—but something,' she said. 'I believe my mother and father are good in everything—it is the child who is tempted.' (Old age was the language, the trembling of youth its voice.) 'It takes a long time to grow up, and as long as they are there I will do as they say. If you could only see that they are good.'

'What makes you think I think they're not?'

'I know you doubt it.'

A light came on in a cottage across the valley but after a few minutes it went out.

She said, 'If you were here longer you would see our ways and then perhaps we could all be friends.'

'If your father saw us together now there would be no chance for friendship, would there?'

'Oh!' was all she said, the other words stumbling and getting lost.

'They have never found out where you go?'

'I am not hiding it,' she lied.

'But if they found out and said you must not do whatever it is you do, would you stop?'

'Of course,' she said, her voice trembling.

'And that would be good?'

'That would be right,' she answered.

'Would they understand?'

'I do not think so, but only because the fault would be mine in not being able to explain.'

'Will I understand?' Morgan asked.

'I think so—oh I did not mean it like that at all. Dear, dear! It is just that I do believe you know the wrong things only because you have not seen . . . I mean somehow you know something . . . They say,' she said, brightening, 'a little knowledge is a dangerous thing.'

Morgan smiled in agreement. 'A little knowledge is all I've ever had.'

Then the words came bubbling from her. 'Oh this is not what I had to say,' she said. 'I always say the thing I've just finished thinking. Two days ago I thought you were full of error. I do not know why but it is something in your smile and how you blew your cigarette smoke. I felt sure that you were wrong all the time. What I've been saying now has pressed heavily on me for two nights and now I do not believe it any more. Perhaps it is only different you are, and not in error. I had not considered before that there could be two ways.'

Her hands were to her cheeks and her head was turned away.

Morgan picked two closed blue flowers and offered one to Mair. In quick confusion she took it. He stuck the other flower in his buttonhole.

Now they were under the trees. Although the sky was lighter, down under the trees it was night. There was a wet smell and their feet slid on the moss. Morgan put out his hands before him, and Mair, a half-step ahead, gave him her hand. The child's hand. Her hair seemed to shine, and there was a lightness to her walk.

They were walking the path he had taken alone the day he had gone to the falls. They went through the clearing with the dead trees, past the quiet punchbowl, beyond where he had turned back, to where the path divided. They took the path away from the river, followed it half-way up the side of the ravine and then parallel to the river. The sound of the river's fall was muffled by the trees; farther on the trees thinned but the falls were then behind them. Across the river the bank had become a curving cliff with three trees growing from its face. The lightening sky had turned the river to silver. Mair stopped and leaned against a tree, and Morgan, panting, stood next to her. He reached for a cigarette but she stopped him.

And then the birds began to sing.

And he was ashamed of his thoughts, come in a woman's voice . . .

Birds, where have you been to learn such song? What have you seen? Not what I have seen.

Are you welcoming the day, or merely laughing at the night?

The sky is a large place for such a small creature: I, so engulfed, would be able to say nothing.

You are instruments, that's what you are: something sings through you. (Birds sing like Bird sang.)

Weeping but no sadness: never a sadness with no weeping.

Suddenly a man's voice rang out . . .

'There is, I remember, a story of how peace returned to the Honey Islands.' The voice was thin and high but with melody and great drama. The words came without strain as if spoken to a child at his feet yet they must have come from across the river.

'When Lludd was king of all Britain,' said the man across the river, 'it was a time of rejoicing, for he was noble and generous. The walls of London were rebuilt, and within them merchants built palaces of great splendour. Banners were hung, trumpets sounded, and the country prospered. But after fourteen years of peace three plagues fell upon the land.'

Mair sighed and held the collar of her coat tightly about her throat. Below them a tall man in a wide hat came through the trees and sat down upon a rock.

'The first plague was an invasion by a race called the Coraneied and their money was fairy money which turned into fungus after payment. No plan to destroy them could be made for the wind, treacherous as a serpent, would take the softest whisper straight to the ears of the invaders.

'The second plague was a scream that was heard throughout the land every Eve of May. So fiercesome was the sound that it took away men's vigour and women lost their loveliness. Crops withered, and old men lost their minds.

'The third plague was a great mystery, for every time the king prepared a feast and celebration, no matter how elaborate, neither food nor drink remained after the first night's revelry.

'At this time, Llefelys, the king's youngest brother, was the ruler of France, and because Lludd respected his counsel and loved him more than all others, he made plans to go to him. So a fleet was prepared and he set sail, and his brother, hearing of the ships, went out to meet him. And on a ship at sea they met and embraced, and Lludd told Llefelys of his troubles, and Llefelys gave him counsel.

'First the young brother had made a horn of bronze so that he could speak to Lludd away from the telltale wind. But words, one to the other, were not easily heard because a demon, lodged in the horn, confused them into mere noise. But wine was brought and poured through and the horn was cleansed and the demon was swept away. And Llefelys was able to speak to his brother, and his brother was able to hear.

' "I will give you certain insects," said Llefelys. "Some of these insects should be allowed to breed for future use. The rest should be squashed and mixed with water. Then all the peoples of the land, Britons and Coraneied alike, should be called together, and the solution should be sprinkled on everyone. Your own people will be unharmed but the Coraneied will be destroyed.

' "The second plague is caused by the red dragon fighting the white dragon. They must be stopped for now is not the time for the red dragon to win. So find you first the exact centre of your island and there dig a pit. In that pit place a tub of the finest mead and cover it with a silken cloth. Stand guard and in time you will see two earthbound monsters fight. They will change into dragons and fight in the air but will tire, and, in the shape of two little pigs, will fall onto the silken cloth and into the tub of mead. They will drink of the mead and fall asleep. You must wrap them up and lock them in a stone coffer in the strongest place in your dominion.

' "The third plague is caused by a giant of great magic. With wondrous music he puts all to sleep and steals your meat and wine. Remember this and have nearby a tub of cold water and into this tub do you jump whenever your eyelids droop wearily."

'Lludd embraced his brother and thanked him, then returned to Britain. And Lludd prepared the magic water as his brother had directed, and called together the peoples of the land, and sprinkled the mixture on all their heads. The Coraneied withered away and were no more yet Lludd's own people were unharmed.

'And Lludd ordered the island to be measured and the exact centre was found to be at Oxford, and there was dug a pit, and in the pit was placed a tub of mead and over the tub was placed a silken cloth. And he set himself down to wait. As his brother had predicted the monsters appeared and changed into dragons and fought in the air and turned into little pigs and fell into the tub and were asleep. King Lludd bundled them up and safely placed them in a stone coffer on Mount Snowdon.

'Lastly, on a summer night, the king prepared a great feast. He dressed himself in his finest armour and carried his mightiest sword. At his side throughout the feast was a tub of cold spring water. When revelry was at its highest a sweet song was heard and Lludd felt his eyes begin to close. Up he jumped and into the tub and there he stayed until he was sure that he would not fall under the spell of the music. Then into the hall strode a giant in armour carrying an enormous hamper into which he started to stuff all the food.

'Lludd shouted his challenge and drew his sword and fiercely they fought. And only after a long battle did the giant fall, and call for quarter. And the king gave it and gained a devoted servant.

'Thus it was that the country was rid of the three plagues, and gained again the time of peace.'

Before the tale was ended the day had come. Shafts of light slanted through the trees and the crown of the hill had turned to gold. The birds sang on with all their hearts, and across the river in the curve of cliff, on a ledge that ran across its face, sat a man, alone, with his hands cupped to his ears.

★　　★　　★　　★　　★

On the way out of the woods Morgan saw the sister figures before them and Mair waited to let them go ahead. Then, in silence, Morgan and Mair walked through the trees and across the valley. Mair stopped sometimes to pick mushrooms that were fresh and firm with earth sticking to them. Once they surprised six rabbits with white fannies. On the west slope of the valley, a brown and white dog moved the ripples of a flock.

When they came to the short cut to the village, Morgan stopped.

'I'm going this way,' he said.

'You are not coming for breakfast?'

'No.'

'You are not upset by what you witnessed?' she said.

'No. Not upset. Puzzled, yet for once I don't have any questions handy.'

'I thought it was a good idea . . .'

'It was. And if it weren't a secret I'd hope for a talk with you before I leave. But I've made arrangements for a full day.'

She stood with her head down, half-turned away from him.

'Thank you for taking me,' he said.

'What you saw,' she murmured, 'was not . . .'

'It could only be good,' he said.

'I do not think he knows we listen,' she said.

And, not knowing what to say, he just said, 'I'll see you before I go.'

Grave-faced, she said good-bye, then went up the hill towards the house. Morgan turned away towards the sea.

And now the day was bright.

CHAPTER ELEVEN

BUT THEY did not want to talk about it.

'I have a passport to his country,' said Will, 'but I only know a few words of his language, so why should I ask him to explain what I would not understand?'

'You speak his language,' Morgan said to Gwylan. 'You tell me.'

'Sometimes it is your language I think I do not understand,' she said.

'Careful,' he said. 'I'm kinda tender.'

'I've only got one world,' said Will, 'and Twm Shon's got one. That is our trouble. Caradoc and Gwylan have many. I do not know what you've got, boyo, one or few or all.'

'I see things all the time that to me are crazy,' Morgan said. 'What else can I do but ask questions?'

'We cannot *understand* everything,' Gwylan said.

'You know the story of the lady of the castle,' said Will, 'who was awakened by a tapping on the window? Well, she gets up and opens the window thinking it was her lover, but in flies a vampire, part man, part bat, part whatever. Flap, flap, flap, around the room it came. Go away, she said, but flap, flap, flap, circling her it continued. So she picks up a crucifix and held it before her and said Vampire, Go Away. But the vampire chuckled and went on flapping, and said, "Thet von't do you no goot, ledy." '

'Oh, Will, that doesn't sound like one of your jokes,' said Gwylan. 'There's no laughter in it.'

'I remembered it from long ago,' said Will.

'This is supposed to illustrate something?' said Morgan.

'It just came to mind. When I am miserable in my own world I laugh at all those in the others. I sort of hope it leaves them helpless because I do not respect their symbols. And sometimes it does leave them helpless.'

'Look, man, I'm no threat. I'm not laughing,' said Morgan.

'I know. But you will see Twm. He is just a man anyone can see good in.'

'Is he all there?'

'Are you?' Gwylan countered.

'You're jumping me again, love,' he said. 'All I mean is —he's a surprise. He stands there talking—to no one, as far as he knows. I guess I like to put a tag on things. He's just not as I imagined him to be.'

'And he is not as you now imagine him to be either,' she said.

'It is our fear that makes us lose our fun,' said Will.

'And our love for you makes us fear,' Gwylan added.

'I am just curious as to what's inside him . . .' But they did not want to talk about it.

'Now here is one more like it,' said Will. 'See there was this man drunk as a full toad and he was going home from the pub on a winter's night, bitter cold it was, so he decides to take a short-cut through the cemetery. Down through the rows of graves he staggers, and oops!—down he falls into a grave just dug for tomorrow's coffin. Down he falls, but up he cannot get for the hole is too deep, the earth too crumbly. Oh get me out, get me out, he shouts, but no one hears. So he waits and waits and a cold, cold hour passes. Then he hears footsteps. He shouts again get me out, and a little old lady looks down into the hole. "Oh I'm cold," said the man. "Well no wonder you're cold," the old dear said before leaving. "You've kicked all your dirt off."'

Gwylan went to Morgan and smoothed his hair and tucked at his shirt, and put her arm around his neck.

'It's never too early,' said Will, watching them.

And they were together again.

It became a long morning, with frequent smiles, of sitting over toast crumbs, talking. By the time they were ready to start for Twm's place, the midday tide was coming in.

Slowly they walked along the beach watching what turned up, stopping to pick up stones to skip them into the waves, stopping to look in holes and to stamp on seaweed pods and to drop things into the hearts of flowering anemones. In the warm rock pools they hand-chased tiny devil fish and gentle shrimp, and caught little scuttling crabs, red and yellow, black and green, tickled by their frantic legs . . . Will lying all the way, outrageously, as if to trusting children happy in their trust; he keeping their attention so that they sat in puddles and stepped in pools.

When they finally got to the break in the sea cliffs, the sea had closed in behind them. White-flecked dark water coursed into indentations and left for a spell quivering spume on grey popping sand: it broke over rocks, refreshing the water in the farthest pools, joining one to another.

They climbed up through the break in the sea cliffs and on up through some rising meadows filled with yellow flowers. On a hill before them were three oaks and it was towards these that they had been walking. From the top of the hill Morgan could see the cliffs-of-the-singing-birds through which the river went on its way to the sea. Will and Gwilan had stopped for breath and were facing the other way. Morgan turned and saw, nearby, a square, once-red bus up on blocks. It was in a hollow the landward side of the hill. Around it spread blackberry bushes and against it grew an apple tree, green and white as ghosts of all fruitions. Smoke from a dying fire came up in a wisp from a stone firewall, and beyond the firewall was a patch of vegetables.

Getting up from the steps leading to the bus was Twm-Shon-the-mole. His ferret was streaking away across the grass, with an occasional burst of quick leaps, towards a clump of gorse.

'We've brought a friend,' Will shouted.

The blind man raised a hand in welcome and when they came nearer he extended it. The hand was cold, the grip not firm. His blue lips were parted as if for breath. His sunken eyes were covered with a film the blue of milk.

'An American,' said Will, 'come for a visit. His name is Morgan Johns.' The grip tightened.

Twm Shon had a long, sad-but-brown face with egg yolk on his chin. Hair thinly fringed his head and his mottled scalp shone. His lips moved but no words came. Thin, he stood with a slight stoop and with a hand like a bird's claw before him. Over a collarless shirt and under a waistcoat he wore a sweater with elbow holes like rosettes.

'Morgan Johns!' he finally said, wiping a hand across his mouth. 'Back you've come then to see what the world is like.' The voice was as it sounded near the river but now there was a tremor in it, and it sounded smaller. Years spent, time watched with concern, strength slipping away, yet for an old man living alone on the top of the wild world, he seemed competent and fit.

'Hello, Twm,' said Gwylan, kissing him.

'Haven't seen you for weeks,' he said. A hand went up to her face, his fingers now his eyes.

'We brought mackerel for lunch,' she said.

'Lovely,' he said. Then he turned towards Morgan. 'Would you like to sit indoors or out, Mr Johns?'

'Oh, in the sun.'

Twm lowered himself to the steps with a sigh. The others sat in the grass. 'I do not have many guests,' he said. 'I suppose peculiarity breeds contempt.' When he smiled his lip hooked over a gap in his yellow teeth. 'And what brings you to Dyfnaint?'

Life is like this, Morgan thought. So many people come in late, want to know the plot, trample over your feet, slow down the play . . . but he told him.

'And did you find him?' Twm asked.

'No one even remembers him.'

'What you might call an unforgettable person.'

'He didn't leave much of a mark.'

'Perhaps it is that you are just not a very good investigator.'

'Maybe. And maybe I didn't really want to find him,' Morgan said. 'I'm leaving tomorrow.'

'Ah yes,' said Twm, nodding. 'The reluctant voyager! At terms with failure before you even set sail.' But it was not in mockery.

'I wouldn't know him now, anyway.'

'People change,' Twm said.

'That's it,' Morgan said, then looking around, 'Looks like the bus service is kind of uncertain.'

'Buses!' exclaimed Will, settling himself facing the sun and closing his lids. 'They should all end up on hilltops.'

'This site was chosen for me,' Twm said. 'One day, when I was about sixty years of age, I decided to run away from home. So I bought the bus and I bought a harp and off I set. I was a timid driver and it took me a long time to get this far. Perhaps this was indeed where I was heading. One evening, daydreaming, I drove off the road and into the river—over my bed there is still a large dent which fits snugly into the small of my back when I sleep on my side. I got wet but that was all. I was very scientific at that time, I even had a map, so I walked downstream to the village. On the way I saw this place. It was just as easy to pull the bus here as to get it back up on the road.'

'Have you been happy here?' Morgan asked.

'Oh . . . ! I have known happiness. Would you have been happy here?'

'I don't think so,' he said.

'I have forgotten what it is like to be young. To be young in heart is not the same at all and I am no more young in heart. I imagine a craving to be moving about, and like a misery I want to say that happiness does not begin with the desire to be somewhere else.'

176

'There's beauty here all right, but there's nothing to show what time it is.'

'That is so—there is nothing.'

'Nothing but you, Twm,' said Gwylan.

'I wonder. Perhaps my hermit days are over,' he said. 'Youth says you must journey to the mountain top but not reside there.' He turned to Will with a straight face that mocked his words. 'Do you think you could get my house down to the beach near you?'

'Aye,' said Will seriously, opening his eye, keeping the glass one lidded. 'With two horses. Pull you down Saturday, find you a woman Sunday . . .'

'I have her.' He, with a sweep of a gentle hand, embraced the valley and the hillside and the small meadow.

'You should have made room for another,' Gwylan said.

As if not hearing, he slowly shook his head, and softly said, 'Over twenty years I suppose I have been here. It is not right to hear not the voice of man when you turn for it. It is right to be near the sounds of the earth but not to shut out man. That is my only sorrow. Before I came here I thought that the human voice was an ugly instrument played by people who could not read its special music. Perhaps I would still decide so, yet I feel sad when I speak to Cyfarthfa and I hear no answer. I am very old now and I cannot remember what was true about my life, or what was false. I tell myself tales. I talk to myself and am glad when I reply. I do not think that I am an idiot yet, but when a man lives alone he loses track of what things are. At one time I was almost learned, but then it was that I likened myself to an idiot under the tree of knowledge haphazardly picking the blossoms from the heavy branches and leaving them jumbled to rot in the basket: with no feet on the ground, no desire to sort and arrange the blossoms to form a profound picture of beauty. Now I focus, perhaps, on a too-small moment—but at least my basket is not in confusion. I don't regret, mind you, that once-upon-a-time confusion—I still remember all sorts of stories from all sorts of books and I like to say them. There is a song they make, Mr Johns.'

'Call him Morgan,' Gwylan said. Twm held open his arms and she went to him and put her face against his. Then she moved away, and arranged the coals for cooking.

'There is wonder in those tales, Morgan, and deep stirrings,' Twm said. 'Why are they not read today? Perhaps it is because of the unfamiliar pictures. It is unfortunate that the other world is so far away. Sometimes I wish that I could have the magic of Merlin or Math the Wizard, then I would receive you differently. I would then know when you approach and I would be prepared, and would do things for you.' He turned to face Gwylan at the fire, leaned forward on his knees, and continued. 'As it is recorded: "Well," said Math, "we will seek, I and thou, by charms and illusion, to form a wife for him out of flowers. He has now come to man's stature, and he is the comeliest youth that was ever beheld." So they took the blossoms of the oak, and the blossoms of the broom, and the blossoms of the meadow-sweet, and produced from them a maiden, the fairest and most graceful that man ever saw. And they baptized her, and gave her the name of Flower-aspect.'

The red ferret popped up out of the bush and stood watching, alert. No one but Twm moved and soon the ferret came and jumped onto his knees and stood there twitching until the old man quietened it with his hands.

'And do you feel that you have wasted some of your young life in looking for this man?' Twm asked.

'Everything has its compensations,' Morgan said, smiling at Gwylan who sat nearby, her knees up, her skirt to her ankles. She, not returning the smile, dropped her head on her brown arms, her face towards the sea.

'Was he friend or was he enemy?'

'A good friend to a boy. He was pretty big to me.'

'The disillusionment must have been a great pain.'

'I don't remember suffering, though I knew soon enough that no man could be that big. He never let me down.'

'How nice to travel so far.'

'My old man pushed me. He was full of bad ideas.'

'Why did not your father come himself if it was his idea?'

'He died.'

Twm dropped the ferret to the grass and clapped his hands, sending it back to the bushes.

'Did he die a happy man?' Twm asked.

'Does anyone?'

Twm sighed. 'And so you came, but not to stay.'

'Tomorrow's the day.'

'Suppose I were your man. What would you say to me?'

'I don't know.'

'You travel all around the world to see a man, and when you meet him you have nothing to say! But perhaps it would be different if I really were your Grando.'

'We were close at one time, he and I.'

'Then it would not matter much if you could not find the words.'

'Anyway,' said Morgan, 'I was to listen rather than talk. Go get wisdom, said my old man.'

'It is a mistake many make. They think that because a

man is old he must be wise. Even if one does have wisdom it is not easy to dispense . . .'

Will suddenly said, 'When you know something and someone wants to hear it, you always find yourself talking of something else.'

'Yes, I would have felt sorry for your man had you met him,' said Twm.

'When I was a boy I was satisfied with a story.' Suddenly awkward, Morgan groped for a cigarette, threw one to Gwylan and one to Will and stuck one in the corner of his mouth, acting tough. 'Like a cigarette?' he asked Twm, as an afterthought.

'No thank you,' Twm said, then, 'Yes, I would. I have not smoked for many years.'

Morgan pulled a cigarette half out of the pack and touched it against the blind man's hand. Twm took it and put it between his thin lips and leaned forward. Morgan held out a match: the flame was not reflected in the old man's eyes. Morgan touched the cigarette with the flame, and Twm inhaled.

'Your father and this Grando were good friends then,' Twm said.

'They quarrelled and never wrote to each other after we went to America, but at one time they were good friends. He wanted me to bring Grando back to America.'

Twm laughed a crackled laugh—an unused sound. 'What a difficult time you would have to persuade an old man to leave his home. New voices, new sounds. A new culture. Some people get too old for change at twenty, but everyone at eighty is too old for change. They are making preparations for death. Preparations are not unpleasant—yet death is the greatest change.'

'But no need to fear death,' said Will, happy to be butting in. 'There's nothing to it. My mother and father are dead. My mother's father is dead, my mother's mother is dead. My father's mother is dead, my father's father is dead. All of 'em dead and not a murmur from any one of 'em. It must be all right.'

'Shush!' said Gwylan.

Twm inhaled again and blew smoke out, twitching his nose like a rabbit, before handing the cigarette out to Gwylan who took it with a smile and dropped it in the fire.

'Did your father alter after he went to America?' he asked.

'I don't know. I was young when we left. He became prosperous and had some prominence in the community and he praised America, and I guess was not too unhappy. He just didn't have much integrity. Maybe this bothered him.'

'It seems so necessary, at times, to remould one's father, just as it does to mould one's son,' Twm said.

'Yes.'

'Do you think that Grando would have changed?'

'I suppose.'

'How would he be, do you think?'

A scarab beetle, green with black markings but gilded all over, climbed Morgan's shoe and fell off onto its back, its legs waving rhythmically in the air. Morgan, not knowing why, reached down with his cigarette end but stopped in time, in shame, and turned it over with his thumb. He lit another smoke from the nub of his last.

'He'd be a composed sort of man,' he said, 'with books everywhere near him. Rigid though, and unbending. Still getting worked up over the conditions in the mines—and in the world. He'd probably attack me for being American and tell me all the things that needed doing in Wales by men of my age. He'd be writing to the newspapers and snorting at the radio. That'd be sad.'

'Why?'

Morgan shrugged, then suddenly sat straight and started to speak but stammered to a stop and changed his mind. Gwylan turned her head to watch him. Twm quietly sat with his head on one side and his mouth partly open like a bird awaiting a crust.

Morgan finally said, 'Why did you leave Wales?'

'I . . . ? Oh I see. But I have not really left Wales. I have just left the twentieth century.'

'Do you remember what it was like before you left the valley?'

'I think so.'

'Tell me what you remember,' said Morgan.

'Of my land? Tell you what I remember of my land? That is an invitation that sends you back until you do not know where to stop. A man remembers from before he existed, and he also makes up prodigiously. For what is it that makes a land? Is it people living in it? Is it legend and history? Is the sea that touches Wales, Welsh? The air above, Welsh? The trees?—no. Yet I used to know the very moment I stepped over the border. I could draw you a line in the grass. In my young days I would say Wales is the profit Welshmen make, the living they enjoy, the glory they cherish, the decisions they act upon. But oh! I could show you where the boundary was all the same.

'What is it that makes a Welshman is another question for you. Pure Welsh am I, some say, meaning who-knows what. What is a Welshman anyway? A Celt some say, but surely also Egyptian, Jew, Frenchman, Dane, German, Briton, Spaniard, blue-eyed Saxon and, without a doubt, a touch of the black man. But if you know precisely—does it make you happier? For what are the races of man? You come back, Morgan Johns—as an American? To do what? To weep a little, stamp your foot and say this is my soil from which I did spring? Does a warm and wet part of you say that these are my people? . . . Oh I hope so, silly as it is . . . But you must remember a Welshman is also a liar and a braggart and a daft talker and a crazy poet and a drunken preacher. Will tells me he is someone you cannot trust with your wife. He once was famous as a robber and a warrior . . . and part of me says how happy I am that he was, though another part is equally glad that he is no longer. He is different in some ways and similar in others. He, like all the rest, accumulates habits and passwords and trappings and badges for he cannot bear madness when unclothed.

'What then is a land? (Establish your position, I used to say when young.) It is a people, locked in by mountains or big rivers, or oceans, or by problems, that grow differently. It is an inbreeding, sometimes creative, sometimes destructive . . . This land has seen the fermentation of a wondrous fruit, and the brew is different from that across the river. Don't ask me if old brew turns bitter . . .'

'Already I know the answer to that,' Morgan said.

'Do you now?'

'But of the Rhondda,' Morgan said. 'What do you remember of the valley?'

'I remember my youth more clearly than I remember yesterday,' Twm said. 'Where I came from every man was a miner at one time or other, and every man remembers the mines. The man without the blue scar was a stranger to the valleys. I was always the stranger . . .

'What was it really like beneath the earth? Do I remember it well? As a boy whimpering to a feeble light that fluttered from the tin helmets like leaves of fear, nursing a smashed finger throbbing in its leather stock. As a man feigning indifference to the creaking timbers, the clatter of falling rock. Sitting down with black-fingerprinted bread and lard, sharing a can of cold tea with a pink-lipped butty. And oh the pleasure in smelling a little bit of hay in the underground stables and the feel of warmth of a pony. Yes, who knows who has not descended what it was really like beneath the earth. And then the long walk to the cage and the long lift up to the face. "Still a bit of light on the mountains, Emrys," and "Aye," Emrys would reply with a cough, "there is a star, look-you—must have been a lovely day." The earth to the men of the valleys was a place into which white men burrowed and white-eyed black men emerged. They seldom saw the sun—oh you know all this. Everyone says they know this. There were no trumpets from the earth, and birds forsook the Rhondda. What song there was was mournful and sung by men.'

'I heard a man say birds do not sing in Dyfnaint,' Morgan said.

'Poor man.' Twm held out his hands as if to hold something, then went on.

'What were we digging for down there, I ask you? Stretched out on your side scrabbling deep in the age-old smell, with so much pain and so much fear, and so much weariness, would it not be nice if what was dug out was shiny and with shape and was yours. But it was only so much weight, so many tramfuls. All that delving was not for you.

For whom? It does not matter. All that mattered was that all the men digging in the darkness of the earth were digging not for their own treasure. There was no choice. All were poor—no tut-tut now—all were alike. Yet there was wealth coming out of the mines. Castles were built with this black money and men felt bitter. Harbouring this bitterness, how did we ever find the price of a smile?

'What did we do with our heads down there? With what did we keep our minds occupied so that we could forget the salt in our eyes and the dust in our throat? Our thoughts were of cold milk and days off with Rugby games, evenings with greyhounds and singing contests. Always the round-and-round thoughts of getting an easier level, a better seam of coal, hoping for the foreman's job. Never thinking of leaving the pits. Our thoughts were of familiar things and a little more luck—they were limited, as if we knew our places. Now, here, for me, the stars are not the limits for my fantasies, but then I was afraid to dream; I dared not wish. Action was planned down there but seldom carried out, for a man has more courage in the dark. Even the strikes were made in an orderly fashion, by sullen nonentities. How I hated our servility and our fear for the man with the dove-grey spats, the shiny hat and his pink fingernails. And my hate accompanied me and held my time down there. Rise up I knew we had to, and I hated above all the men who, because of their coughing children and their love for them, would not act with strength. For some, courage is easy; standing for what is right is too difficult.

'For what is fear? Each day you meet it, pushing it from your mind, until some days you do not even know what it is that makes you sick. Down, down, the cage goes, talk gets less, breath shallow. At the bottom of the shaft the dust is like smoke (though in the lamp you see it tinted like a dark rainbow) and for ten steps you do not breathe at all.

'What did we encounter down there? What were our devils? It is said a man who meets and conquers fear must change. How does this fear change you I would like to know. Day after day so that they could work with their fear, yet there was no change. Watch the pit-head faces after an explosion. Horror is there. If facing fear changes a man what does facing horror do? Horror one day in ten—does that change you too? And yet it was not fear that drove men from Wales. It was a weariness. Men were tired of empty stomachs, tired of seeing skinny children with transparent skin get to be the right size for a three-foot level, tired of seeing a wife weeping because a man had one beer at a penny a pint, tired of coal dust on their phlegm, tired of the family requiem. Tired also of losing their temper and going out on strike only to return three months later for less than what they had when they struck.'

Briefly he touched the corner of his milk-blue eyes.

'No,' he went on, 'no one should blame your father for leaving Wales.'

'I don't blame him,' said Morgan.

'You blame him for something—forgive me, I am playing the old blind mystic. But sometimes I blame myself, and I can feel for your Grando. He seems silly now, not speaking to a friend because he could not change the man's mind. Each man has to choose his own way and Grando stuck his nose in. Most people are guilty of that. Everyone thinks that he is right, that his is the only way. Yes, I know how he felt. Had we all stayed, perhaps virtue would have been rewarded. I believe it often is. Perhaps what we did wrong was try to change the system instead of changing ourselves . . .

'And how did they leave? Some men left the valleys with fear, some with courage. Some tried to find something going forward, some by going back. A few looked for it in their own day. A good, sad, friend ran to London, I ran to Dyfnaint, your father to America. The Lord knows where your Grando ran to. The sad thing is that miners, often, took nothing with them to their new environment. And is it not funny—it would seem that if you counted all the people who ran away you would expect no one today in the valleys, yet still full they are. But have they left their mark there?—those who stayed. The slag heap is a bit steeper, I suppose, and I hear they now have pit-head baths.

'What does a man want? That was a question that used to fester in me. I am surprised at the bump-bump of my heart when I ask it again after all these years. What does a man want? Poverty does not enrich a man's soul. It is fine to work for what is lacking, and a poor man has plenty that he lacks, and many things he wants, and this they say is a challenge. But Man should be most concerned with the want for a place of calm. There has to be a place which is his own. He must find it. It is easy for me hiding in the hills? Yes it is easy for me. I came to the mountaintop straight from the depths—that was my luck—and that was my trouble. But what I do know is that man never knows what he wants, never knows what he needs. Man only knows the desire to occupy his days to the fullness of his appetite . . . If I were not afraid I would like to go back just to see what has been done.'

'Changes have been made,' said Morgan. 'Men still sing sad songs, but the miner seems confident.'

Twm shook his head. 'Then someone must have stayed. I ran away. I even accepted a new name without protest. But for me it was right: too long have I been concerned about this.'

Will was in the grass, his head cushioned in his arms, and his one eye moving, tennis-fashion, from Morgan to Twm as they talked.

'What is your real name?' Morgan asked.

'Gwyn,' Twm said quickly. 'Gwyn Lloyd.'

Gwylan and Will watched him as he answered, but they said nothing.

'Then I'll call you Gwyn,' said Morgan.

'No. I like the name Twm. Perhaps some day when I see more clearly . . .' He rubbed his hands over his face. 'What would I have liked to have done with my life? There is a question for you. I have planted a tree and it has given me pleasure.' He cocked his head towards the apple tree at the side of the bus. 'I used to wish for blossoms and fruit on the branch at the same time—that was when I had my eyes. Now I know that too much at once is more than enough . . . I have not fathered a child. I wish I had, but I have not, not in any way. No child has come from me . . . I have now no more wish to fight a beast though I suppose I have been fighting one throughout my life, and he is still there. But the time of truth does not come every day. Yes I would have liked to have done other things with my life but I am not sure what . . . All those fears! I thought light would dispel them. And where is there most light, I asked. Yes indeed, up here. Earliest in the morning, last at night. And then I lost my sight. Is not that strange. If I were my own God (and only sometimes I think I am) I would have liked to have kept my sight. Blind people often call their blindness a blessing, but I am not strong enough all the time to consider it a blessing. Sometimes, when I am calm, I say it is sad that it happened so late in my life for I have not much time to face all I now do see, but calm moments are rare. I would like to see you, young man, and you, Gwylan. The sight of Will I can do without.' Will chuckled. 'I would like to see the birds that sing; I would like to see the river. I would like to see again a dragonfly—my mother believed they came from the devil. Run she would . . . I would like to see all these hills.'

'What made you leave home?' Morgan asked.

'Believe it or not, one fine Sunday in the middle of summer a bird came down to sing. "Hello bird," said I, "where you from?" He sang on and the Rhondda was transformed—but not for long. The chapel cat got it as I watched. Quick silence. In the fifty years I'd then worked in the mines I had seen many men die in ways as horrible as that, but I bitterly mourned the little drab bird that came down singing from the mountains. The next day the strike began—a strike that I had partly brought about. The big wheel stopped turning, the trams were silent, and men stood around the *Red Lion* with unfamiliar clean faces, and with white mufflers tucked into waistcoats . . .'

'The *Red Lion*?' Morgan mused, his eyes screwed up.

'Or some such name. There are *Red Lions* in every town in the Rhondda.' But he did not go on with his tale.

'Talk, talk, talk, nothing but talk in me,' he said. 'Questions, oh the questions that are in my head . . .' then '. . . It has been a quiet day. I cannot even hear the sea.'

Gwylan handed out an assortment of dishes and an assortment of implements. There were two mackerels apiece and potatoes roasted in the coals and fresh mushrooms and crusty, buttered bread. Gwylan put a kettle of water on the coals before joining them. The skin of the fish was crisp, and the flesh firm.

'It is amazing what civilization can do, Twm,' said Will. 'These are the first fish Morgan has caught in twenty years.'

'I am the same,' said Twm. 'It is amazing the things man thinks he has to do. Some day I would like to go fishing again.'

'Tomorrow,' Will said. 'I will come for you.'

'Say yes,' said Gwylan.

'Perhaps,' Twm said.

For the rest of the meal Will talked of the fishing he had done or was going to do. ('Willie, you are a sailor as long as you keep one leg on firm ground,' teasing from Gwylan, and his reply, 'The sea is the sea two inches from the sand.') But when the plates were clean and the tea had been poured, Will had less to say, and when he stopped, all talk stopped.

The hill they were on seemed to be the only one in the world, for the horizon on the land side was treed and the mountains were hidden. They had not seemed to climb much from the beach yet the sea, now cloud-shadowed, was flat and far away.

There was no other world. What he saw now was unchanged from the time the sea dyke burst—and that was as long ago as legend. A man here with dim eyes at the tips of his fingers, and in his ears only the sighing of the wind and the sighing of the sea, this man can only believe what his senses tell him. And what is brought by the senses has been here for many a thousand summers.

'Do you play a flute, Morgan?' Twm asked.

'Yes.'

'Then it was you by the river.'

'I saw you and tried to call but the roar from the falls was too loud.'

'It was a strange melody.'

'I was improvising, y'know.'

'That is what I like to do,' Twm said.

He got up and went indoors and came out carrying a tall, covered harp. He uncovered it and set it at the bottom of the steps and leaned it towards him. It was a faded gold with a dragon curled along the spine.

'A virtuous wife, a fat cushion, and a tuned harp, they used to say, is happiness,' Twm said, tuning it.

'When I was a boy,' Will said, 'there were harps in every pub, and in the summer at every seafront.'

Twm, seeming to pull away each note into the palm of his hand, picked out a gentle tune. He played the melody four times and although each time it was different, the difference was subtle. When it was over he touched the strings obliquely with his open hand, and the sound was of a soft wind through the strings.

He waited and no one spoke, so he played again. The song was *The Bells of Aberdovey* and he played it simply, and when it was over he ran through a few pretty, corny, bars like bells. Then he got up and covered the harp and carried it back into the bus. No one objected and no one offered to help. And when he was gone, still no one spoke. He stayed inside for the length of a smoke.

When he came out Morgan said, 'I used to know that song when I was a boy. There's not much I remember but I now remember that.'

'Then I do not think that your journey was a waste,' said Twm.

'No.'

'I am glad that I bought that harp. I used to laugh at myself for I said the harp is within you. But this one happened to help me find mine.'

Lunch had been taking well over the hump of the day and the sun was already touching the night clouds over the sea. Cyfarthfa appeared again, scratching himself. A twittering came from the branches of the three oaks; darkness seemed to congregate in patches about their leaves.

'What is the sunset like?' asked Twm, his blind eyes to the sky as if listening for movement.

Will and Gwylan seemed not to hear so Morgan said, 'Like the dying down of a fire.'

Twm nodded as if remembering. 'Lovely sunsets we have sometimes,' he said. 'Sometimes fearful. I used to be afraid of the dark so my mother would say, "If it were not for the sun's death you could not see what you can see with a candle; what's in the dark you can see better without the sun." But that used to make it worse—some part of you always regrets death. It seemed to me, and I told her so, that you could see more with your back to the dawn than with your face to the sunset. She understood me all right but I never understood her.'

Gwylan got up and put her arms around Twm's neck and whispered in his ear. He nodded, smiling, then got up and held out his hand to Morgan.

'I am going in now,' he said. 'I am very glad you came. Do not forget us.'

'I won't. Not this time.'

Hesitantly, Twm said, 'If you decide to stay longer, come and see me again. Such a chance I had to find out what you were like and all I did was talk about problems that have come back from long ago, about fears that I thought had long since gone. So, you see, I, though old, am not wise—no more than your Grando is wise. The world should love a man in failure. But there are more pleasant things to talk about had we the time.'

'It was a pleasure,' Morgan said, uncomfortable at the formality in his voice.

'Time for now is gone,' Twm said.

Morgan struggled but could say no more.

Then, quickly, lightly, Twm placed his hand on Morgan's face—before turning away and going into the bus.

Willie got up and stretched. 'Go on down, you two. Twm keeps brandy in the house for a cold, and I can feel one coming on.'

Morgan said, 'In case I don't see you, Will . . .'

'Aye, you old bastard. Spit in the ocean for me when you cross.' They shook hands, and Will winked and punched his arm. As Morgan and Gwylan turned to go, he said, 'Be happy today, lovies.'

On the way down through the fields (not the way of the beach) Morgan asked, 'What did you say to cut Twm short?'

' "Twm," I said,' said Gwylan. ' "Morgan is leaving early tomorrow and I like him very much." ' She turned away and picked a long grass and started to peel the outer skin.

He put his arm around her and, in silence, they walked to where the path divided.

There, Morgan stopped and, not sure, said, 'Did you ask . . . ?'

'I told him to stay away the night,' she said.

'I'll pick up my bag from the Parrys',' he said. 'Wait for me.'

'Let me go on down. I want to see Maggie, and there are things I want to do before you come.'

'Then I'll meet you at Will's,' he said.

'Yes.'

Out in the open of a hundred hills, yet the intimacy was there when mouth met mouth in a brief, gentle, meeting.

CHAPTER TWELVE

THEN it was evening. Shadows had spread like wine along the valley, and night clouds had blown across the sky. Grasses were moved as if by creatures hurrying home. The sound of birds had given way to the creak of bats. Morgan stopped and looked about him. Darkness was cleaning shabby walls and straightening sagging roofs; the farm buildings formed a firm pattern under dark trees. Through an open door yellow light fell out like grain . . .

. . . Night cannot nibble it, nor can the mouse in the wind . . . The wind, this night, is like the sea; the hills are like the sea. Everything at times like these, these happy times, everything is like the sea (not the sea sailed upon). The night comes with the wind, as does the sound of sea, as do the shape of hills. All good comes with this wind, as with this wind some good will leave.

> *The gentle wind,*
> *The arousing thunder.*

I leave with one; I came, awakening, in the other. Neither

one nor the other in light . . . Here, darkness comes yes like a thief or like a lover, creeping, and the shadows of men thrown here and there around the edge of it take on its character: here and there around me are the shadows of long-ago thieves and long-ago lovers. No one, surely, now walks before me across the yard between shed and barn— only the shadows of those who come with the night and with the gentle wind? Yet it seems as if . . .

One of the dogs barked then recognized him and came wagging with its head down. Morgan stopped and spoke to it, and the other dog came up for a word and a thump.

Parry appeared in the doorway. 'I have been waiting for you,' he said. His shadow, thin-legged, big-bummed, with elongated head, filled most of the square of light on the ground.

'Even the worst of us gets a productive day, once in a while,' Morgan said.

Parry came across the yard and swung a walking stick against the rumps of the dogs, quickly one-two, sending them yelping away.

Morgan straightened and said, 'Make it brief, 'cause I'm in a hurry.'

'Ah, an act of discretion is it,' said Parry. 'But can you go far enough, fast enough, then?'

'You got a riddle, Parry? Maybe you want to spread it out before I go.'

'Maybe, indeed, as you say,' said Parry.

'Then let's have it. I've got a few answers that might fit.'

'I am not surprised at all that you want to leave,' said Parry, making faces. 'And it is no news to me that you are leaving, for if you were not going of your own accord I would throw you out by force.'

'What's up your arse?'

Parry shook his stick. 'Don't you dare put on that act with me. You and your filthy ways! Oh I can read behind your face as if all the dirty words in the world were written there.'

'That's a slip, man.'

'You know what I mean.'

'I haven't a clue. What rubs you rough is some imagined thing, I guess, but what it is I wouldn't know. And I don't give much of a damn. I've got prettier things to worry about.'

'I ought to put the law on you. I might do it yet.'

Morgan shrugged. 'Wouldn't be surprised you could find something to fit.'

'You had just better leave my house before I lose my temper.'

'You've lost that for keeps,' Morgan said. He went to pass by, and Parry raised his stick and shook it, but when Morgan stopped and waited for more he lowered it again. Still he thrust forward his head pugnaciously and raised his voice.

'I've got a good mind to give you a good thrashing, anyway,' he said.

'Full-of-jokes Parry! Do you know what you're talking about?'

'Ho! Mr High-and-Mighty-and-Innocent,' Parry said, wagging his head. 'I know your kind. I suppose you think that I do not know what you were trying to do with my daughter this morning.'

'You know, huh?'

'Oh, I know.'

'What happened?'

'I know what you wanted to happen. You a grown man, and with a little girl.' His voice raised to a woman's pitch, and Mrs Parry came to the door.

'That is enough, Llew,' she shouted. 'Llew! That will do. Come on in now. No use . . .' He turned and snarled, 'Go to bed,' over his shoulder, and she closed the door to a crack.

'You've got a head like a bucket,' Morgan said. 'There's little point in saying it but I will all the same. I asked your daughter to walk with me on my last day here for a pure and simple reason. One maybe you wouldn't understand.'

'I understand well enough.'

'I did not touch her . . .'

'I know. I know. I took her to our doctor. But that does not mean you did not try something. Oh I bet you tried something.'

'You took her to a doctor?'

'Yes.'

'Like you think this right?'

'It was for her own good, and for our peace of mind.'

'What kind of Charlie are you?'

'Ask, indeed! I am a man who tries to form his children in the image of his father and mother, who brings up his daughter to be good and pure and believing in all that is true. My daughter is as pure as my mother was.'

Morgan farted his lips.

'And if I had not succeeded in this upbringing you would have violated her.'

'You know, if you were not so dumb . . .'

'I give you warning now.'

'Oh shut up!'

Parry hunched his head into his body and raised his stick again. Morgan waited, hoping, but Parry lowered the stick and turned and walked, muttering as he went, towards the house. The square of light from the kitchen door was now narrowed to a yellow finger pointing out into the night.

Morgan waited, only to avoid walking side by side. He was a dozen steps away and behind when he saw a movement in the doorway of the shed, and a man quickly come out, carrying a stake. The man stepped between Morgan and Parry, raised the stake and thudded it down on Parry's head. Parry's knees bent, his hands flipped up as if in resignation, and he crumpled without a sound. It was the man who had struck the blow who gave out the cry.

Morgan, rooted, watched the man throw down the stake and spring back into the shed, before he was able to run to Parry. He turned him over and looked him over. Seeing that he breathed, he stepped over him and went to the doorway of the shed. Little light reached past the doorway and he could see nothing.

'What was that about, friend?' he said quietly.

The only answer was a kind of animal snuffling to his left. With one hand touching the wall, the other extended before him, he shuffled towards the sound, expecting no trouble. The man, hunched in the corner, did not move when he came upon him, nor did he stop his weeping. It was Emlyn, his face in his hands and his head against the wood.

Morgan put his arm about his shoulders. 'Hush,' he said (a word not used for years). 'It will be all right.'

'Killed him, killed him.'

'Not him. He's too tough.'

'Kill him, kill him.'

'Stay here until I come back. And be quiet.'

'Don't go.'

'I'll be back,' he said as a scream rang out.

He stepped to the door and Mrs Parry screamed again when she saw him. A hoarse scream it was, scraping up her throat.

'You've killed him,' she cried, curving her fingers like talons before her. She ran to her husband and bent over him, her hands to her face as if in horror, but when she straightened up excitement sparkled in her eyes.

'You did it,' she said. 'You killed him.'

A window flew up and Owen called out in a small and frightened voice.

Morgan took another quick look. 'No one's strong enough to break his thick head.'

'He's dying. I'll have the law on you.'

'For one thing or another,' he said.

'This is criminal, cut and dried . . .'

'Move over and let me get to him.'

Parry had the weight and the rough shape of a double bag of coal. After attempting to lift him, Morgan grabbed him under the arms and dragged him across the uneven yard, guiding the jerking legs away from the potholes.

Rhys and Thomas, mouths and eyes wide, watched from the stairs as he dragged him through the door and into the kitchen. Owen shouted a question from his room.

Morgan lowered him in front of the fire. Waiting, was Mair, and without a word she poured water from the fire kettle and ripped cloth into strips. Mrs Parry ran around in circles, threatening Morgan and crying out at Mair. Morgan, holding Parry's head, and Mair, soaking the cloth, ignored her.

Parry snorted, his mouth hanging loosely, his chin covered with dirt. His scalp was laid open about a finger's length, and blood oozed steadily, darkening one side of his head. The flesh was bruised and torn, and the wet hair was like a creature sucking there. But the full contour of the wound was visible and it did not seem deep. Mair squeezed water over it and pink rivulets ran down his brow and into the hollows of his eyes. His eyelids quivered but remained closed. Mair cleaned the wound, smoothing the hair from it, then held a pad of cloth firmly against his head. She would not look at him while she did this but he saw that her eyes were inflamed.

'You know what you're doing,' Morgan said.

'I saw it happen, so I was prepared,' she said.

Mrs Parry started blubbering.

'Be quiet, Mam,' Mair said.

Mrs Parry recovered and elbowed herself between Morgan and Mair, snorting, 'Well, if my own daughter won't even let me see my own husband . . .' She smelled strongly and her dress was wet at the armpits.

'It is not bad,' said Mair.

'Not bad! He's dying,' Mrs Parry said, a sigh vibrating. She turned to Rhys and Thomas who were staring from the doorway. 'Get out, get out, you staring fools,' she shouted. 'Get to bed.' She chased them up the stairs, and from the door shouted down the passageway at Owen. 'Get clothes on you, Owen. At once do you hear.'

With her mother's increased excitement Mair's head dropped lower so that no chance glance could be met.

'That is more than enough from you,' said Mrs Parry. 'Get your things together. We will see to you, don't you wait. You will see.' She waggled her head and her eyes seemed twice as large behind her glasses; her face was like a mask with a rubber mouth.

'He's all right now,' said Morgan. 'It's a wonder he hasn't had it before.'

At this Parry opened his eyes and groaned, 'Oh my head.'

'That's about all you could expect from him under the circumstances,' said Morgan.

'Wicked and callous you are,' said Mrs Parry.

'How do you feel?' Morgan asked.

Parry looked at him with some surprise, then his eyes went wildly about the room and he sat up, and, in one surge of vomit, swooshed all over the floor.

'Get the doctor,' Mrs Parry cried to Mair.

'I had better go,' Mair said to Morgan.

'Don't dare speak to him,' said her mother.

Mair took her coat and left, as Owen came to the kitchen door. Mrs Parry turned to him like a general. 'And you go, quick, quick, and get Uncle Dewi and the others.' And then, with near delight, she said to Morgan, 'Hoh! Now you are for it.'

'There's no hurry,' said Morgan.

'What's happened?' Owen asked.

'Just say your father's been attacked.'

Owen screwed up his eyes and stuck his tongue through the gap in his teeth. As he watched his father spewed again.

'Coo! What a mess,' Owen said.

'Shut up,' said his mother.

'I'll be done when you get back, Owen,' Morgan said.

'Don't answer,' said Mrs Parry.

Owen, at the door, vacantly looked first at his mother,

then at Morgan. Morgan tried out a smile. The boy, serious, barely acknowledged it with a raised arm before leaving.

Morgan climbed the stairs, and without looking at Rhys and Thomas, went into his room and lit a candle. He noticed that his hands were shaking yet there was laughter close to his lips.

He packed in a few minutes, then sat on the bed. The room looked so very familiar, as if he had lived there for years. Oddly, the memories were pleasant; good things had happened here. Brown wood, brass bedstead, quilted bed, noisy candles—all would soon be part of the established past. He blew out the candle and stood for a moment at the window looking out at the hills and the few, far, country lights. Then he picked up his bag and left the room that had been his. In the outer room the two hired men sat side by side on the double bed as if in the back seat of a bus.

'Well, Thomas. Well, Rhys,' he said. 'Good-bye now.'

'Good-bye,' said Rhys. Thomas waved a shaking hand.

'Be friends with the boy,' he said, 'and blast and bedevil his dad.' But they could not return his smile. They were still afraid, and still-and-always-would-be lost.

In the kitchen Parry was sitting on a stool with a basin on his knees, a wet cloth wrapped around his head.

'Now's your chance,' Morgan said. 'You can keep your brains in the basin. They've never been much good to you.'

'Don't you worry,' Parry said hoarsely. 'You won't get away with it.'

'Maybe you and I get what we deserve,' Morgan said.

'Then say your prayers.'

'Yeah,' Morgan said, on his way to the door. 'I'll remember you in them.'

He walked across the yard and poked his head in the shed. 'I am leaving now,' he said, not knowing if anyone was there. Suddenly arms were about him and Emlyn had his face against his coat. He was not crying though.

'He won't die,' Morgan said.

'Oh!' sighed Emlyn.

'And he doesn't know it was you. Do you understand? He thinks I did it.'

'I will tell him.'

'No. Let him think that.'

'He is bad,' Emlyn said.

'He cannot hurt you.'

'I know. But he thinks he can.'

'Piss on him,' said Morgan.

'Oh the faces he makes.'

'Yeah. And some of them stuck. I bet that isn't the first time he's been saved by his thick head. Go in now and go up to bed. And say nothing.'

'You are going away?'

'Yes.'

'I'm all right.'

'Sure,' said Morgan.

'Good-bye then.'

'Good-bye, Emlyn.'

'Friend you were.'

Without looking back, Morgan hurried through the gate and down the path to the dark woods, and through that, following the clear twisting path of the stars above. His feet caught on stones and roots, and branches sometimes brushed his arms, but he knew the way now. This was not home to him, would never be, yet the night air seemed alive with spirits that he knew, and he was glad that they were with him.

As the path came out of the trees he stopped to look upon the village. Is this the last time, he wondered. Are these good-byes? That is home out there across the sea— the sea that's sailed upon. That was home. That he knew now well. But suddenly, so soon it seemed, this visit was ended just when regrets were gone. Oh say all good-byes twice or more. Say them for all the times you did not say hello.

In the village, more lights faced the hills than faced the sea, for no one lived in their living-rooms and the living-rooms faced only the street. The lights were pretty but to-night the village had no shape: haphazardly went the lights up a hill, along the beach and around the cove. The street lamps a line of whiter lights that pointed to the faintest light of all. The railway station. The way he had come; the way he would go. The way home.

Morgan shifted his bag to his other hand and stuck the tip of the flute into his pocket, keeping it there with the pressure of his arm, and went on down. Near where the path met the road he saw Mair returning. He slowed down then stopped to await her.

She came on slowly and he saw that she cried. He stood awkwardly as she stopped before him and really let go. She dropped her hands from her face, fisted them at her throat and, lips blubbering, eyes shut, she cried up at the sky.

He touched her hands, then held them as if to warm them. No longer composed, with no attempt at woman, the girl cried on and on, and he said nothing until she choked over her crying and her coughing stopped her. Then he held her shoulders and she dropped her head and cried anew, but softly now.

'It is your innocence, child,' he said, remembering.

'What is happening to me?' she cried, her forearms tight together at her chest. He tightened his arms but was unable to say what had been said, long ago, to him.

'But I feel as though I have done something bad,' she said.

'So do I, but neither of us have.'

'I am so afraid,' she said.

'And I cannot say not to be,' he answered. ('Oh, Maggie, Maggie–love, what shall we, shall we do–oo.')

'It is awful the change that has come about in these two days.'

'I did not bring it, Mair.'

'Oh yes you did. But then no blame is there in that. It had to come sooner or later. I think that I was happy though when I was able to avoid all trouble like this. Now I am so afraid.'

She shook over a sob but the tears had stopped. He gave her his handkerchief, and she blew into it, then threw back her head and stepped away from him, her hands stuck in her coat pockets.

'Where's the doctor?' he asked.

'There is a child being born,' she said. 'The doctor will come as soon as he can.'

'It's often like that,' he said.

'You are going now?'

'To friends.'

'You must hurry before my uncles come.'

'I'll be all right.'

'What an awful day,' she said, 'and it was such a lovely morning.'

'Don't forget Twm Shon,' Morgan said.

'No.'

'Well then . . .'

'It was nice knowing you,' she said.

'I'll remember you well,' he answered.

'You will?'

'Yes indeed.'

'I am glad.'

He held out his hand and she took it and they stood for a moment without moving. Then she said, 'I was so ashamed of what my father did to me. He shamed me and he shamed you.'

'He hasn't much love in him,' Morgan said. ('Throw, man,' he remembered from somewhere, 'then wait for the tinkling of your own glass.')

'I hate him but I can't stop loving him. I have loved him too long,' she said.

'At least it shows he can't always be right. You've got to make up your own mind from now on.'

'I will,' she said in an unsure voice.

'And who knows—your love may change him.'

'I feel that love is not nearly so powerful as I felt it was yesterday,' she said.

What could be said to that!

'Good-bye,' he said.

'Good-bye,' she answered.

And she kissed him. Her lips were cool and her tearful kiss was like a child's, and for a moment he wanted to call after her and hold her, and cry along with her a bit, and say that everything would be all right. But he did not. For he could not.

And he let her go, crying again, on up the path towards the troubled house.

He watched her until she was lost in the darkness, and listened until her footsteps stopped sounding. Then he moved on.

No light shone from Will's cottage so he slowed his walk, breathing deeply the salt air, hoping to dissolve the hard stone in his stomach. The tide was out and the river slapped plip-plap against the quay.

A summer night, yet two ago was winter.

He crossed the bridge and left the quay and walked the few steps along the pebbly beach to the cottage. He knocked on the door not expecting an answer and not getting one. The door was unlocked and he opened it and slipped his bag inside and placed his flute-case on top of it, as one would do in a waiting-room. Close to home now, but there was waiting to be done. He went outside, closed the door, and started walking to meet Gwylan.

Then he stopped.

Is everything as it should be?

Listen!

The plip-plap of the river water, the rattle of the sea stones, the squeak of the moving boats, the gentle wind . . .

And look around!

A light sea mist rolling against the cliff, the lighthouse winking on, the white-touched water, the village lights like frightened yellow stars hiding in the brown night . . .

plip-plap   plip-plap   plip-plap-plip

Way, way up the valley a lonely light shone—a shepherd? As far away as company, but peace is farther still.

plip-plap

You knew it all the time didn't you!

Everything was as it should be. Everything was in its place.

Five men stood like dark statues across the only way to the village. Five men like dark heraldic beasts. They stood, evenly-spaced, across the bridge: if he tried to pass two men, without moving, could touch him. Without moving, they could link hands and form a barrier, could form a chain. Five men like beasts across the one way to the village. They made no move, but their stillness did not weaken the threat.

Maybe they would do no harm—but oh they could. No thieves, no lovers these, but men happy in the darkness of the night.

Five men like statues. Three for uncles, two for the fun.

Morgan hunched his shoulders nervously, clenching and unclenching his hands. Behind him the quay curved and came to an end over the water-splashed rocks. The beach stretched endlessly to the right—an empty beach dark for deeds, a sea, ever-moving, eager to cover them up. The village street quiet, with empty yellow stars. Morgan blew through his lips but no whistle came. He waited, breathing deeply, his hands now hanging loose.

No place to go but on. But when he stepped forward he set them in motion. Step by step, he and they, moving closer two steps at a time.

The man on the beach side of the quay bent, picked up a rock and lobbed it towards him. He did not see it in the air but it fell short and the thud of it gave a hint of its weight.

Morgan, retaliating, picked up a rock . . . ('if they make

you feel like a saint, Charlie, take a prophet or two with you') . . . and threw it. Two men moved apart and the rock fell between them—he was against the sky and they could see it coming, while they were against the dark of the hills. His throw started another man throwing. The rocks, the size of fists, now thudded close to him, some landing behind him and rolling over the edge of the quay into the river. One rolled against his foot and he picked it up and pulled back his arm, but changed his mind and tossed it over the side.

And it plopped into mud.

He turned to see where it had landed, and as he did so a rock struck him on the shoulder. He spun round in pain as two more rocks landed close by.

They were now just twenty steps away.

Running back to where the boat was moored, Morgan jumped down into it. Steadying himself a moment he jumped out across the river, landing to his knees in water. He fell forward onto his hands, recovered, and in two steps was out on the mud and running across the tide-out harbour. A glance showed the five heading back down the quay to cut him off but he was up the iron ladder and running down the street towards the *Rose and Crown* before they were across the bridge.

Almost immediately he sensed the good start dwindling. Out of condition, he could do nothing about the slowing of his legs. He had trouble getting air in and out and it tasted of blood. His throat was congested. A stone underfoot shot him off-balance and he could not recover his missed stride. Faltering, he rounded the curve—and ran into Gwylan.

'Panic,' he panted, a thumb pointing over his shoulder,

the grin a failure. Before them stretched the one street with all the houses and shops joined together into one, long, unsymmetrical building, the *Rose and Crown* a long hundred steps away. They could hear the clatter of boots just around the curve.

Morgan turned to meet them but Gwylan took his hand and led him a few running steps to a door which she opened, ran through and closed behind him.

It was a dark and damp covered alley that led to a back garden. They ran down it, passed two side doors, into a garden smelling of mint. Gwylan pulled up her skirt and clambered over the low stone wall into the field beyond. Morgan followed and they waited, crouched in the dark, listening. A clatter of feet sounded—and stopped. Then the sound of a doorlatch, and down the covered alley came one man, fumbling and uncertain. When he got to the garden they crouched lower but Morgan was now ready. As he was about to rise and face him a light came on in an upstairs window and someone shouted a hello. The light put them in light but also chased away the man in the garden before he was close to the wall to see over it.

With his breath recovered, Morgan took Gwylan's hand and started along the bottom of the hill field, behind the row of houses. As they walked he told her what had happened.

She stopped and when Morgan had finished she said, 'The garden of the *Rose and Crown* is over this wall. Shall we go there? There will be pushing and shouting, I suppose, but Constable Richards is there, and also people you know.'

'And what do I say? If I keep Emlyn's name out of it I'm in a hole.'

'I didn't think of that.'

'It would be easier just to leave without facing them.'

She did not answer.

'Twelve hours won't make much difference.'

'It is half a day,' she said.

'You can cross the ocean in that time.'

She turned away and stood on her toes to look over the wall into the garden.

'Show me the way to the road,' he said.

She put out her hand and took his, and led him on up the hill.

★   ★   ★   ★   ★

When Caradoc opened the door he greeted them with a laugh. 'Four feet all over the shop,' he said. 'All colours; born today, barely dry.' Near the fire was a box full of kittens and the overlapping mother blinking and rumbling up at them.

'It is always the same,' Caradoc said. 'At the last moment she decides that she does not want the box she always uses. Frantically she searches, this way, that, upsetting things, calling out. Then with a blink and a sigh she settles down and out they come—plop, plop, plop, etcetera—five this time.'

He knelt at the box and made noises at the cat, then stood up and thrust his head back.

'What a wonderful place is this world, this world we have,' he said. 'Oh what a world we have—is not that wonderful. What a day it has been as if to prove it. For me no need to use my memory. No thoughts of what was gone, or what was coming. A day of squirrels, rabbits, mice and pussy cats, oaks and spiders and dewdrops and rooks and willows, and a fragrance of the earth. Everything in

212

movement, and in peace. It started with two birds sitting together on a branch like pine cones, and they sang to me the morning long. And I went out and the cat went out but they did not move. I wonder what they said. Oh what a day it was . . . marred only by the impudence of the voice box. Brrrr-brrrr—scared me out of my half-wits. "Ello," I says, holding it five feet away and standing on a chair to stop getting electrified.' He laughed again, his face red. ' "You must telephone your report in more often," came the voice with no nonsense. "But I am afraid of the instrument," I said to them, "and everything I say into it comes out contrary." '

'You'll have to pour wine down the tube to drive out the demons,' Morgan said.

Caradoc opened his eye wide in pleased surprise. 'Well, indeed,' he said. 'You got something of what you came for then.'

'I suppose so.'

Gwylan smiled, but at no one.

'I'm told that for some people even the beginning takes years,' Caradoc said.

'For me too,' Morgan said. 'I've been here ages.'

'Hardly a moment.'

'As much as I can take anyway.' But he laughed at himself as he said it. 'I'm leaving tonight.'

'You saw him?'

'Yes.'

'He's out of your system?'

'I wouldn't say that much,' Morgan said. 'But, you know, time goes.'

Caradoc shook his head and turned to Gwylan. 'Would you like a kitten?'

'Perhaps,' she said.

'Soon they will open their blueberry eyes,' he said, 'and that is the time to press for promises from people who say perhaps. A week beyond that they will be raising ructions.'

The cat turned over to get at another soiled foot, and the kittens squealed and realigned themselves—a fuzzy ginger one, like a caterpillar, at the tail, a grey one next, then a black, a mottled one, and a tabby near her throat.

'How many fathers for this lot,' Morgan wondered.

Thin, pointed tails quivering, the kittens nudged each other out of the way, the ginger one forcing the mother to lift a leg as it got lost. Then just when the others had found a place again the ginger one took off on an expedition up and down the line, under and over and between the others, disturbing them. At the end of the line it sneezed three times and the others took advantage of its preoccupation to grab back at a nipple.

'Welcome to the world, feller,' said Morgan. 'Don't look so mad, for it isn't that bad.'

Gwylan smiled at him, dropped her head briefly to his shoulder, then moved away. Caradoc looked at her with concern, but said nothing, and merely moved the kettle onto the coals.

Morgan picked up the ginger kitten, the mother watching and making take-care noises. The kitten opened its tender pink mouth and snorted for breath as it blindly struggled, its hairlike claws tickling like the legs of a captive fly, its legs spreadeagled and moving but its body not supported by them, its head jerking in imbalance like a weighted toy crocodile.

'I know just how you feel,' Morgan said, smiling.

But then a cold breath from the open door touched his

neck and he spun round with one hand fisted, expecting trouble. But the door was closing, not opening. And it was closing on Gwylan.

'Where're you going?' But the door was shut on the question.

'Everyone seems concerned about their home,' Caradoc said.

In his hurry Morgan could not unhook the kitten's claws from his coat. 'I guess I didn't make it clear,' he said.

By the time he had put down the kitten, and had opened the door, Gwylan was at the gate. He called to her and she stopped, but only for a moment, and then was gone.

'Wait,' Caradoc said to Morgan.

'Later . . .'

'She is like my child.'

'I want her with me,' Morgan said.

'Nothing is that easy,' said Caradoc.

'What d'you mean? I know my mind.'

'Saying that the decision is made is sometimes the easiest part,' Caradoc said.

'Right! But I know. Now I've got to talk fast.'

'Talk with me instead. Give yourself time.'

'Time!' Morgan glanced at his watch.

'The train does not leave for an hour. In Dyfnaint you can find anyone in five minutes.'

'I hope anyone can't find me in five minutes.'

'Come and have some tea,' said Caradoc.

'Tea! Everything, even tragedies, stop for it. But do those off stage know we've stopped for it?'

'Come on in,' Caradoc said, holding onto Morgan's sleeve.

Impatience showing, Morgan went back inside the house.

215

But when he closed the door and saw himself in the mirror, he remembered something, and the urgency left. For he had been here before. Not two nights ago, or winter if now be spring, but ages before ages ago. And even that thought had been thought before—ages ago. When did it all start, he wondered. I now know what I am about to do . . . and, (when done) . . . that was it. But so nearly not . . . The gleam of lamp beyond my shoulder, the frame of gold, light below darkness above. I look at myself and for the first time what I see does not displease me, neither the weaknesses nor the strengths . . . Two nights ago there was not but now there is—a white and blue jar with a fat curve and a small lid and the markings like the patterns of birds in the sky. It fits the palm remember? And someone said it is to put all things ugly that might not be so later. Remember a cool curve in the warmth of a summer day. Oh remember? Water streaming with summer noises. Bird song. Sunlight. And I did things beautiful that day. Long ago when things were different. Yes, I remember. That was innocence. Can be again? Don't ask too much. Now I know I miss that day. Memory had almost gone for good.

'Take it with you,' Caradoc said.

'Thanks.' But he could not, just now, touch it. 'Where's your bird?'

'Here,' Caradoc said. He raised his arm and down flew, singing, the green and yellow bird from somewhere near the ceiling, and perched on his finger.

'She needs some little extra loving today,' he said, 'because of all the excitement.' And he pushed saliva from his tongue and the bird chattered as it drank from his lips.

Morgan said, 'Hello bird,' but it did not come when he

216

held out a finger as a perch. Caradoc moved it to his shoulder where it settled to comb its wing with its beak.

Caradoc prepared the tea then, pouring it and sprinkling herbs into the cups as he had before. He held his cup with both hands and sipped.

'You are right,' Morgan said. 'No time at all has passed since the night of the storm . . .' The bird flew to his shoulder and nestled up close so that he could feel the cool, smooth wings against his cheek . . . 'but a lot has taken place.'

He then told him of all that had happened in the day.

When the story was told, Caradoc said, 'I would like a tunic made of the night sky with all its stars, so that when I wear it I am God and when I discard it, I am man.'

'Grando wanted to welcome me as a wizard.'

'It is our weakness.'

And also your strength. He remembered it but did not say it.

'So not sorry were you to find your Grando,' Caradoc said.

'No.'

'You were not looking forward to it.'

'Perhaps not.'

'So now you've seen him. And that's that.'

'It happened before I knew it.'

'But long enough, you suppose?' Caradoc said.

'We missed a lot when we talked, but . . .'

'But you have so little time?'

'That's it,' said Morgan.

'Life is like a river—always changing its shape. But sometimes it seems to take for ever to reach the sea.'

'Not mine.'

'So concerned are some people about handling the boat, they do not watch where the river is taking them.'

'Everyone worries about the current.'

'At one time or other,' Caradoc agreed. 'I have an advantage for when the river nears the sea its path is not so confined and the current is not so insistent.'

Tentatively Morgan put his hand up, but the bird did not move so he stroked it. 'Grando does not feel as you do, I don't think,' he said. 'Sometimes he seems to regret his old age, only sometimes to enjoy it.'

'I do not think that is true. Perhaps you brought sadness to him.'

'Don't you think he fears what the last days will bring?'

'Oh apprehension is there sometimes, but no fear. Your Grando told me a lovely thing once. He said something like . . . "When I used to see, out of the corner of my eye, the falling of a leaf it would fill me with sadness. The wind would come and the leaves of the forest would flutter like a million birds in anguish—so I thought. But with my sight I also lost the sadness. Now, when the trees are bare I love the feel of the clean branches, and I remember a pretty dignity." . . . No, I have missed it.'

'Do you think he's spent his time wisely?'

'What a question for a stationmaster! There is something fine about a struggle, yet success is suspect sometimes.'

'Has he been happy?' Morgan pressed.

'Happy! Glad I will be when you leave with all your interrogations.' He smiled. 'Did you ever hear of a man who had too much happiness. This man you knew is content—more or less. As I am content—more or less.'

'Why didn't you tell me about Grando?'

'You seemed so strong. You seemed agreeable enough but we loved Twm Shon. And at the time he needed love more. When you knock down a moth, the gold on your fingers is worthless, and then you have nothing.'

'Everyone certainly trusted me,' said Morgan.

'We took you at your own value!' said Caradoc.

Morgan finished his tea; it was cold but he shook his head to the offer of more. He glanced at his watch and stood up, shooing away the bird to the mantelpiece.

'You are in a hurry to go?' Caradoc asked.

'I always seem to be in a hurry.'

The bird flew up to its cage, and went in.

'It is easy when you travel alone,' Caradoc said.

Morgan agreed.

'When you really know you have someone else, life slows down. Perhaps, for you, that is not yet to be.'

Morgan did not answer. He went to the box of kittens and crouched before them. They slept, twitching in their young dreams. The mother twisted her head so that he could scratch her neck, and when he did so she closed her eyes and pumped her feet against the side of the box.

'What are you going to name them?' he asked.

'Those who choose them have the right to name them,' Caradoc said. 'I just describe them.'

'Yeah,' Morgan said, subdued.

'While I remember,' said Caradoc. 'Let me punch your ticket. I often forget.'

Morgan took out his ticket and read it.

'Anything with writing and dates on is so confusing,' Caradoc said.

'It's good for another month,' Morgan said.

'Sometimes I punch the wrong side so it looks as if

you have gone before you have come. How I got this job I cannot remember, but I am sure I did not get it honestly.'

'How many hellos can you say in a month?' Morgan asked.

'Oh thousands, and say them twice over too. How-d'you-dos are fine in their place. Particularly to yourself.'

'Crazy,' said Morgan, smiling.

'In a month you can even paddle upstream a bit. Not for long, not for ever, but you can look under a few bridges.'

He put away his ticket-punch, blew his nose, and stood for a while with his forehead against the mantelpiece, looking at the fire.

Morgan took down the blue and white jar and raised the lid and poked a finger at the things inside. There were buttons and badges and seeds, an old watch and a whistle, coloured stones and pencil stubs and seashells, a bardic ribbon, and a monocle. Morgan stuck it in his eye and said, 'Pip-pip!'

Caradoc said 'Pip-pip!' also, and added, 'It's plain glass.'

Then he put on his coat, lit his lantern and went to the door. 'I must set the signal,' he said, 'and wave on the train.'

But he was back before the train came. 'There are three men come for you,' he said.

'Oh Christ!' Morgan stood up and rubbed the back of his neck. 'What happened to the two-for-fun?'

'They say they mean to hurt you but they won't kill you.'

'What about diplomatic immunity?'

'When you cease to be just an observer you are bound to suffer pain.'

Morgan looked at his watch, and then at Caradoc.

'Do not look at me,' said Caradoc. 'I am too old.'

'I know,' he muttered. 'And I left my book at home.'

'Your book?'

'Yeah—my hero book.'

The train whistle sounded, and Caradoc went outside with his lantern.

Morgan went to the door as the train came steaming into the station. As it stopped, its weak lights fell from dirty windows onto an empty platform. No one got off; no one was on.

The three men stood just outside the gate with the WAY OUT sign.

Caradoc, as far away from Morgan as were the three men, had a carriage door open, waiting, the whistle to his lips.

'Let's hear it,' Morgan said.

Caradoc slammed the door and blew his whistle. The train moved away and picked up speed. The three men came through the gate.

'And so, instead of ending, now it begins,' Caradoc said.

'You can start the bread poultices, any time you like,' Morgan said.

'Pain does not last for ever.'

'No,' Morgan answered, and the smile was not forced, 'it just feels that way.'

Caradoc put down his lantern, and, as he turned to go, he recited—quite loud:

With Masters of all Unicorns,
Past dark heraldic beasts,
Pain and humiliation comes
Oh! long before the feasts.

Morgan waited, between two pools of light, one red one green, and he heard the door close as the men threw down their caps and held out their hands towards him.

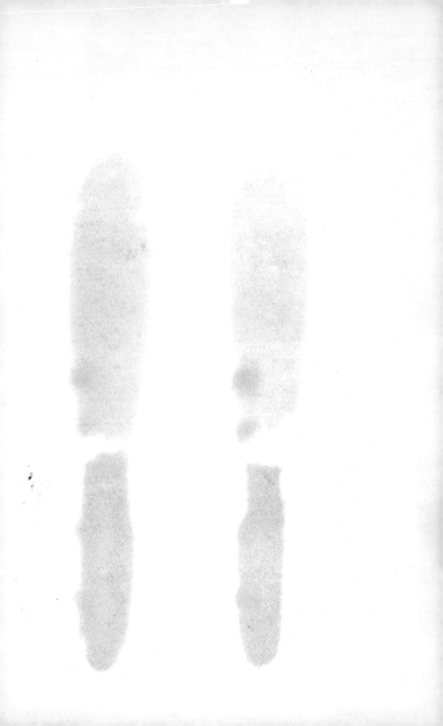

DATE DUE
